HIGHLAND STORM

HIGHLAND CHRONICLES SERIES - BOOK 1

ELIZABETH ROSE

Barbara!
Enjoy & have
a great holiday season!
Elizabeth Rose

ROSESCRIBE MEDIA INC.

Cover created by Elizabeth Rose Krejcik

Edited by Scott Moreland

ISBN: 978-1690993704

AUTHOR'S NOTE

Since my stories span the generations, I am listing a quick family tree that you can use as a reference guide when reading this book. To find a more in-depth family tree line please visit my website at ***elizabethrosenovels.com.***

Cast of Characters – Family Tree:

(Highland Storm features the hero, Hawke MacKeefe and the heroine, Phoebe MacNab)

Callum MacKeefe (Hawke's great-grandfather)

Ian MacKeefe (Callum's son and Hawke's grandfather – MacKeefe Clan Chieftain)

Lady Clarista (Ian's English wife and Hawke's grandmother)

Storm MacKeefe (Ian's son and Hawke's father)

Lady Wren (Storm's English wife and Hawke's mother)

Renard (Hawke's older half-brother)

Lark (Hawke's older sister – her son is **Finlay**)

Hawke (Hero)

Heather (Hawke's younger sister – her son is **Liam**)

Angus MacNab (Phoebe's father and MacNab Clan Chieftain)
Phoebe (Heroine)
Elspeth (Phoebe's younger sister)
Agan (Phoebe's younger sister)
Miles (Phoebe's little brother)

Onyx MacKeefe (One of the Madmen MacKeefe and Ethan's father)
Ethan (Hawke's friend)

Aidan MacKeefe (One of the Madmen MacKeefe and Logan's father)
Logan (Hawke's friend)

Ian MacKeefe (One of the Madmen MacKeefe and Caleb's father – not to be confused with Hawke's grandfather, also named Ian)
Caleb (Hawke's friend)

Orrick (Sorcerer first seen in *Legacy of the Blade*)
Euan and Lennox MacNab (villains)
Osla (Phoebe's cousin)

CHAPTER 1

SCOTLAND, 1385

Hawke MacKeefe balanced his foot on the body of his attacker, pulling his sword from the man's chest. Three bandits lay dead at his feet never having assumed Hawke would be able to kill them all. He wished he hadn't had to do it, but the odds were against him. His life had been threatened and he had no other choice. Any good warrior worth his salt would have done the same.

Wiping the blood from his blade on the clothes of the deceased, Hawke scanned the surrounding area for more. The woods could be filled with men lurking, just waiting to attack any unsuspecting traveler or hunter they found. Three of Hawke's good friends were out there somewhere and he only hoped they were safe.

Preferring his solitude, Hawke often broke away from the others during their hunting trips to still his thoughts and clear his mind. Didn't every loner crave time to himself? His friends were often boisterous and noisy. Especially Caleb, who had a tendency to laugh and talk too much for Hawke's liking. It only managed to scare away the game and make Hawke's head hurt.

He'd just slipped his sword back into the sheath when the warning cry of his red tail hawk from above told him he wasn't finished yet. The bird swept down as Hawke spun on his heel to see another man emerging from the brush. With vengeance in his eyes, the assailant shot forward with a sword in each hand, meaning to kill him. Hawke unsheathed his blade with a sigh, ready to protect himself once again.

Apollo, Hawke's bird of prey, always accompanied him on the hunt. The bird often helped him ward off attackers on the road as well.

With another shriek, the red tail clutched the man's hair with its talons, managing to draw blood. It was all the distraction he needed. In one motion, Hawke sank his sword into his assailant's heart.

"Damn it, canna a man ever get a quiet afternoon to himself?" growled Hawke, retrieving his sword as the man fell to the ground, dead.

Chaos seemed to find Hawke wherever he went. He was naught more than a silent storm followed by a wake of destruction that was left in his path. Not by choice, of course, but done out of necessity. While Hawke's blood always burned for a good battle, he didn't want one unexpectedly and neither did he like having to take on so many men at once by himself.

Ten years ago, Hawke was scarred mentally by a tragic event. Since then, he vowed to do everything he could to protect his clan, especially the women and children. His only regret was that he couldn't do more. Through the years, he'd earned the reputation of being one of Clan MacKeefe's fiercest warriors, following in the footsteps of his well-known father, Storm. Hawke was always in the front line at any battle and he preferred it that way.

He was eight and twenty years old now and had no wife or children to care for. After what happened, he wasn't sure he ever wanted to be married again. Mayhap that was another reason why he was fearless and sometimes reckless.

"Hawke," shouted his good friends, Logan, Ethan, and Caleb as they rode their horses at breakneck speed toward him through the forest. What started out as an innocent hunting trip, sadly ended up as a deadly battle.

"We're here to help," cried Logan, the son of Aidan, one of the clan's members referred to as the Madmen MacKeefe. Logan's blond head turned back and forth as he sat upon his steed with his sword held high, looking for more attackers. His gray wolf named Jack ran silently behind him.

"We heard the attack. Dinna worry, we've got ye covered," the dark-haired Ethan, son of Onyx, assured him. His horse was led by his white Irish Wolfhound called Trapper.

"Ye're too late," said Hawke, heading over to his horse loaded down with game that he had caught on the hunt, aided by his hawk. A half-dozen wild fowl and two hares were Apollo's contribution to Hawke's catches. "I've already taken care of it." He used a cloth from his travel bag to clean and shine his sword, not even looking at the dead men.

"Who are they?" Caleb, the smallest of the men, Ian MacKeefe's son, slipped from his horse to inspect the dead bodies. Hawke's friends were all sons of the Madmen MacKeefe – the Highlanders known throughout the years for doing wild and crazy things. Hawke, on the other hand, was the second son of their clan's laird, Storm MacKeefe.

"Let me take a look." Logan swung his feet over the side of the horse, heading toward one of the corpses. Ethan dismounted and followed. The wolfhound sniffed around the bodies while the wolf stayed in the shadows.

All three of the men stood there staring, not saying a word.

"God's eyes, ye act like addlepated wenches sometimes, I swear!" Hawke pushed his way between his friends and yanked open the cloak of his last attacker to see the bright red plaid underneath. "Bluidy hell, they arena bandits at all."

"MacNabs!" spat Caleb, sending a shiver up Hawke's spine to hear the name of their biggest enemy. The MacNabs and the MacKeefes had been feuding for as long as Hawke could remember. The MacKeefes had tried to put an end to it and align with them ten years ago, but things only got worse from there. It was a time that Hawke wished he could forget but it haunted him still.

"This isna guid," said Ethan, as if any of them needed to be reminded of the fact. Killing a MacNab would only bring trouble to their clan, even if it was done in self-defense.

Logan's wolf lowered its head, slinking forward and growling lowly.

"What is it, Jack?" Logan's eyes darted back and forth. "Did ye hear someone?"

The sound of a horse's hooves trampling the ground came from the thicket. Hawke's head snapped up and he surveyed a small man in a hooded cloak bolting away through the trees.

"I'll get him," said Logan, unsheathing his sword. "Come on, Jack," he told his wolf, turning and heading to his horse.

"Nay, I've got this one." Ethan sprinted ahead of him to his horse. "Trapper and I will handle it."

"What about ye?" Hawke asked Caleb with a raised brow, knowing that each of his friends wanted to prove he was the best.

"They've got it handled," said Caleb with a shrug. Caleb might be the smallest of the friends, but he was faster and just as brave as any of them. He'd proven himself time and again to be a strong warrior. Caleb's only problem was that he was often lazy.

"Ye need a pet, Caleb, like the rest of us," said Logan from atop his horse. "One who can travel with ye and help ye fight."

"Aye. When are ye goin' to finally do somethin' about it?" asked Ethan over his shoulder, turning his horse.

"As soon as I find one that's right for me, I'll get one," snapped Caleb. "Now stop tellin' me what to do."

"Whatever ye say," Logan said with a smirk, preparing to leave. Hawke stopped him and Ethan.

"Nay," he said, holding his hand in the air. "Let the MacNab go."

"Blethers, Hawke, what's the matter with ye?" spat Ethan, turning his horse back to look at Hawke straight on.

"They're our enemies," Logan reminded him with a clenched jaw, always ready for a fight.

"And that's exactly why we're goin' to let that one go," explained Hawke, looking up to see Apollo circling in the sky above his head, keeping an eye on the MacNab. "We are goin' to let him get word back to the bluidy MacNabs that the MacKeefes canna be defeated. Mayhap then, they'll stop tryin'."

"I think you'd take them all on by yerself if ye could, Hawke," said Caleb.

"I did it to save my neck, no' because I wanted to," grumbled Hawke.

"If ye would have waited for us, mayhap we could have taken them as prisoners," remarked Ethan. "Either way, this canna end well."

"Aye," agreed Logan, looking at the dead bodies all around them. "This is goin' to start a battle for sure."

"Och, ye three are simpkins," spat Hawke. "I told ye, I did it in self-defense. Ye werena here and I didna have a choice. And the reason I let the last man go is to prove we dinna hunt down MacNabs just to kill them. We only do it to protect ourselves from havin' our throats slit."

"I hope the MacNabs will see it that way," said Caleb.

"I hope our laird sees it that way," added Ethan, talking about Hawke's father. Both Hawke's father, Storm, and his grandfather, Ian, were chieftains of the clan. This worked out well since the MacKeefes held land in the Highlands and also claimed the Lowland Hermitage Castle on the border as their own.

"Let's get back to the castle since it's gettin' dark," said Hawke, mounting his steed. "I dinna want my horse to twist its leg." They were in the Lowlands now, and the MacNabs were a Lowland clan. However, that never stopped them from attacking in the Highlands as well.

"Shouldna we go through their pockets first?" asked Caleb, once having been a thief in his younger years and still having the urge to steal in his blood. He moved with stealth and had the polished skill of sleight of hand that was admirable even to an honest man. If there was ever a need for someone to sneak in and out of the shadows without being caught, Caleb was the man.

"Nay. Leave them," commanded Hawke. "We dinna want anythin' from a stinkin' MacNab."

"I agree, it is bad luck," said Ethan, being very superstitious. "We dinna want to tempt the fates and bring a curse upon our heads."

"I still say we should –" started Caleb, looking down to a dead MacNab, poking at the man with his toe.

"Nay!" said Hawke and Ethan together. Logan just shrugged his shoulders and looked the other way.

"I'll never understand ye," grumbled Caleb under his breath, climbing atop his horse.

The men quickly headed back to Hermitage Castle with their game swinging from ropes at the sides of their horses. Hermitage Castle was seized by the MacKeefes years ago, led by Hawke's father, Storm. But the MacKeefes weren't a Lowland clan, and divided their time between the Lowlands and the Highlands. However, their presence this close to the border was always a risk. If it wasn't the English looking for trouble, it was another clan who wanted to claim the castle as their own.

Hawke wasn't a man who gave up. He could have easily killed the last MacNab, but he wanted the message to get back to them that they couldn't win. He wasn't even sure why the MacNabs were this far south since their stronghold, Crookston Castle, was up near Glasgow. Riding back to Hermitage Castle, Hawke had a bad feeling in his gut that the situation with the MacNabs was only going to get worse.

CHAPTER 2

When the men rode through the gates of Hermitage Castle, Hawke was surprised to see so many people heading into the great hall. It was already nightfall. Usually by now, the servants were settling in to sleep by the fire and the men of the clan were drinking or playing dice.

"I wonder what all the commotion is about," said Ethan, stretching his neck, trying to see in the torchlight.

"It looks like mayhap we have visitors," answered Hawke, eyeing a horse and cart by the stable that he'd never seen before. "Caleb, go find out and meet us in the great hall with some ales. I'm parched."

"Aye, I will," said Caleb, hurrying away while the rest of the men handed over their horses.

"Have the game warden take our catches from the hunt to the steward," he told the stablemaster.

"Aye, Laird Hawke," said the man, using the courtesy title Hawke gained from being the laird's son. Too damned bad his older brother would most likely be next in line as laird once their grandfather or father passed away. Renard already had sons of his own, and Hawke had nothing.

Hawke looked up as Apollo descended from a darkened sky to land on his outstretched leather-clad arm. The falconer ran out to join him.

"Be sure to give Apollo his choice of the hunt," instructed Hawke.

"My laird?" questioned the falconer, eyeing up the baby boar tied to the side of his horse. "Ye mean, any of the fowl, or the hares only, right?"

"Nay." Hawke ran a finger over his bird's head and the bird clucked in appreciation. "I mean anythin' he wants," answered Hawke.

"But the boar is big enough to feed a guid half-dozen men," the man protested.

"Apollo worked hard today and deserves it," he said, knowing the falconer as well as Hawke's father wouldn't agree. The hawk was a raptor and helped to hunt food for the clan. Hawke had personally trained Apollo, having had his pet for ten years now. The red tail had been abandoned as a fledgling when its mother was killed by an owl. Hawke found the bird and took it into his care. Since then, Apollo never left Hawke's side.

Making their way into the great hall, Hawke and his friends headed over to the fire and stood with their backs against the wall. It was a learned action, always protecting oneself so an enemy couldn't sneak up from behind.

They were all welcome to sit at the dais, but since it was already so crowded, Hawke and his friends often ate at the lower trestle tables instead. Ethan liked to flirt with the lassies and Logan liked to brag a lot. Caleb, on the other hand, usually went from table to table, listening to all of the conversations. He was nosier than a gossipy alewife. Hawke just liked being closer to the kitchen because he could get more food faster that way.

"Who is that man?" asked Logan, trying to see through the crowded hall.

The man he spoke of was talking to Hawke's father, Storm.

Gathered around them were the rest of the men's fathers, the Madmen MacKeefe. With them were Hawke's grandfather, Ian, and also his great-grandfather, Old Callum MacKeefe, who should have been long dead by now, but seemed to live forever. Hawke credited that to the old man's potent Mountain Magic that he brewed in his still ever since Storm was a boy.

"I think there's a young lass with him," said Ethan, looking over the heads of the crowd.

Hawke didn't even notice the girl at first. She was so short that he figured she was naught more than a child.

"I'm no' sure who it is," answered Hawke. "But I can bet whatever they're talkin' about has somethin' to do with our faithers."

"Here comes Caleb, now," announced Ethan anxiously. "He'll let us ken."

"Caleb," called Hawke, flagging him down, hurriedly taking two of the four tankards from the man's grip and handing one to Ethan. "What did ye find out?"

Since Caleb was small and lithe and good at sneaking around, he'd most likely be able to tell them anything they needed to know.

"It seems the man's name is Brigham Ogilvy. He is the King's Chronicler," said Caleb, handing one of the tankards to Logan. Lifting the rim to his mouth, Caleb took a long draw before continuing. "His daughter is with him. I couldna see her well, but I noticed her face was comely."

"Really? What's her name?" asked Ethan, always interested in the ladies.

"Never mind that," said Hawke. "Why did the king send his chronicler here to Hermitage Castle?"

"It seems King Robert wants everythin' recorded." Caleb took a seat atop the table, putting his feet up on the bench.

"What's everythin'? And get yer arse off the table," scolded Hawke.

Caleb scooted off the table, taking another swig of ale before he answered. "The king wants all the heroic deeds as well as the crazy ones recorded of the MacKeefe Clan throughout the years. The chronicler is startin' with your great-grandfaither, Hawke. Auld Callum is tellin' him now how his Mountain Magic is what has kept him alive so long. The chronicler wants to ken everythin' from how Storm MacKeefe caught the band of renegades to how Aidan MacKeefe saved the Stone of Destiny."

"These stories get grander each time they're told," Hawke mumbled into his cup.

"I wonder if we'll be mentioned in the book," asked Ethan, looking over the rim of his tankard as he drank.

"No' unless we do somethin' crazy like our faithers," said Caleb.

"They'll be writin' about yer faither for days, Hawke," said Logan. "After all, he has never been beat in the caber toss yet, no' to mention, he is called the Highland Storm for the way he fights."

"Used to be called," Hawke corrected him, looking across the room at his father. "No one has called him that in years." Storm's long blond hair was cut short now because it had been turning gray through time and he was trying to cover up the fact. He was still a strong warrior and to be respected, but Hawke noticed him slowing down lately.

Storm called over Hawke's older brother, Renard, and they all laughed and talked with the chronicler. Old Callum was eager for them to taste his whisky, passing full tankards of Mountain Magic to both Brigham and his daughter. Hawke almost laughed aloud when he saw the man and the girl take a drink of the potent brew and double over holding their throats. He was sure the Mountain Magic was going to get more than one mention in the Highland Chronicles now.

"What's the matter, Hawke?" asked Caleb. "Ye look upset."

"Nay, that's only his usual look," commented Logan with a chuckle.

"Aye," agreed Ethan. "Hawke is always scowlin' about somethin'. Guid friend, ye need a lassie to wipe that frown off of yer face."

"I dinna ken," said Hawke, running his finger along the rim of his cup. Logan's wolf and Ethan's Irish Wolfhound laid under the table together. Everyone knew and accepted the animals, although the women still seemed a little leery whenever Ethan brought his wolf into the great hall.

"Ye've got that look in yer eye again, Hawke," said Logan. "That usually means trouble."

"Nay, no' trouble," said Hawke, a swarm of thoughts filling his head. "I'd just like to be mentioned in the Highland Chronicles, that's all."

"Hah," laughed Caleb. "That'll never happen unless we can do crazy or heroic things like our faithers."

"We do," said Hawke with a flash of a smile. "But no one ever notices."

"He's right," said Ethan. "The things we do make the acts of our faithers look dull."

"Do ye really think we can get mentioned in the Highland Chronicles?" asked Logan, his eyes lighting up at the thought.

"I dinna care. I dinna need to be mentioned," said Hawke with a wave of his hand to dismiss the conversation. He drained his tankard and plunked it down on the table. "I'm goin' over to meet the chronicler."

"Me, too," said Logan.

"And me," added Ethan, following on their heels.

"Wait for me," called out Caleb, running to keep up as the men made their way over to the newcomers.

"Hawke," called out Storm, motioning for his son to join them.

"Da," said Hawke with an acknowledging nod, approaching the visitors curiously.

"I'd like ye to meet Brigham Ogilvy and his daughter, Bridget."

Storm held out his hand to include the visitors. "The king has commissioned his chronicler to add the MacKeefe Clan to his collection of books. Isna that wonderful?"

"I suppose so," said Hawke, eyeing up the crowd. Not only his father, but also the fathers of his friends were huddled around the scribe, looking over his shoulder into the book.

"I dinna see anythin' about me in there," said Aidan, Logan's father. "I'm sure ye'll want to ken all about me bein' the guardian of the Stone of Destiny."

"Really? Ye guarded the coronation stone of the Scots?" asked the chronicler, seeming very interested.

"He didna mention he let the stone get stolen by a wench," Logan mumbled under his breath to his friends.

"Well, I was able to hunt down and save a Book of Hours for a wealthy English lady," announced Onyx proudly.

"He left out the part about his mathair stealin' the book in the first place, and him abductin' the Sassenach before he even looked for it," whispered Ethan behind his hand to his friends.

"Dinna forget about me," added Caleb's father, Ian, standing taller. "I killed the ghost of a man who came back from the dead."

"Ye did?" asked Bridget with wide eyes, leaning forward to hear more. The girl wore a gown that seemed too big for her, and her hair was covered by a wimple. Only the beauty of her face gave away the fact that she might be older than she seemed.

"If he would have made sure his enemy was really dead when he killed him in the first place, he never would have come back from the grave," said Caleb softly to his friends.

"That's nothin'," spoke up Hawke's grandfather, Ian. "My son, Storm, not only tracked down a band of renegades single-handedly but it's because of him that we were able to lay siege to Hermitage Castle."

"Oh, we want to hear that story," said Bridget excitedly.

"Should we tell them that my da was taken prisoner by a blind woman and that he had the help of two clans and a Frenchman in seizin' the castle?" Hawke asked his friends.

The four of them looked at each other and shook their heads. "Naw," they all said together, knowing it wouldn't be a good idea to point that out.

"Did I tell ye about the squirrel I used to have?" Aidan asked the chronicler.

"Squirrel? Hah, that's nothin' compared to the Scottish wildcat that traveled with me," Onyx interrupted.

"A Scottish wildcat?" asked Bridget, sounding impressed.

Ian cleared his throat to gain the girl's attention. "Did ye ken that I had a wolfhound that drank Mountain Magic?"

"Och, that's nothin'. My deerhound could read minds," Storm said, pushing to the front of the crowd.

"This is all very interestin'. Why dinna we start from the very beginnin' of all these adventures?" asked Brigham, watching closely as each of the men spoke. He seemed to study their faces as they talked.

"The beginnin'? Then ye'll want to start with me because I am aulder than dirt." Hawke's great-grandfather, Callum, stepped forward, holding out his tankard to a servant. "But first, why dinna we all have another round of my famous Mountain Magic?"

"Aulder than dirt? How auld are ye?" Bridget asked Callum.

"No' too auld to still enjoy the smile of a bonnie lass," said Callum, winking at Bridget and cackling like an old hag.

"How auld is yer great-grandfaither?" Ethan asked Hawke curiously.

"I'm no' sure that anyone really kens the answer to that," Hawke answered. "The auld man is goin' to live forever. Well, I've had enough. I'm goin' out to the practice yard to toss a few cabers. Anyone care to join me?"

"Are ye still hopin' to beat yer faither at the caber toss at the Highland Feis this year?" asked Ethan.

"Ye ken no one has ever beat him. He's the champion," Logan pointed out.

"Mayhap." Hawke ran a hand over his jaw in thought. "But this year at the Feis, I will hold the title of the winner of the caber toss, I assure ye. And I dinna have much time to practice."

"Just let it go, Hawke," Caleb told him, shaking his head, making his long, dark curls spring up and down with the movement. Hawke always thought a man shouldn't have curly hair – that was for wenches only. Then again, Caleb was small like a wench, so what did it matter? "Yer faither is chieftain. Let him hold the honors."

"I agree," added Ethan. "It wouldna look guid if ye beat him."

"What's the matter with ye three?" spat Hawke. "If we're goin' to get mentioned in the Highland Chronicles, we're goin' to have to do somethin' to get noticed."

"I thought ye didna care about gettin' yer name in the book," said Caleb smugly. He smiled and crossed his arms over his chest.

Hawke looked over his shoulder at everyone making a big deal over their stories, all vying to be the next mentioned. Mayhap he cared after all, but he wouldn't admit it. "It doesna matter. I just want to win the caber toss, that's all."

"Let's go," said Ethan. "I feel like throwin' a few boulders around. That should rock the boat a little and get them to notice me."

They started to walk away, but Caleb didn't move.

"Are ye comin', Caleb?" asked Hawke.

"Nay, I think I'll stay here," Caleb spoke over his shoulder to them. "I'd like to hear what goes into the book."

"Well, I dinna care," said Hawke once again, heading out of the great hall, wondering what his father would say when he beat him at the caber toss this year.

CHAPTER 3

Phoebe MacNab rode like the wind, hoping against all odds that the MacKeefes weren't following her. Her body trembled and she found it hard to breathe. What started out as a harmless trip to the border to collect healing herbs, ended up being a deadly, bloody battle for her escorts. Why had they decided to attack the lone man? That wasn't supposed to happen. Mayhap it was because he was just one man and they were four. Little did anyone know this warrior fought like four men wrapped into one.

She rode to camp where her father's right hand man, Euan, and some of the clan members awaited them. As she approached, they jumped up, knowing something was wrong.

"What is it?" yelled Euan, drawing his sword and running to her. He was followed by a half-dozen other men of her clan. Not able to find the rare healing herbs needed to heal her bedridden father, they had decided to head back to the Highlands. But in one final attempt, Phoebe convinced a few of the men to take her into a part of the woods they hadn't explored yet, right near the border. Little did she realize how close they were to MacKeefe territory.

"They're dead. They're all dead," she screamed, slipping off the horse and running to meet them.

"Who's dead?" asked Euan's brother, Lennox. The man was battle scarred and had leathery skin. He was a good ten years older than Euan and also bald. Euan had red hair and beady eyes. Both of the men were stocky and not much taller than her.

"My escorts," she said, struggling to breathe and trying to still her racing heart. "They were killed by a man wearin' a purple and green plaid."

"The MacKeefes," snarled Euan. "We'll kill them all."

"Nay!" she cried. "It was the MacNabs who attacked a single MacKeefe. He was in the woods by himself."

"Ye make no sense, lassie," growled Lennox. "If our men attacked a single MacKeefe, why are they dead now instead of him?"

"The MacKeefe fought like a lion," she exclaimed. "I've never seen anythin' like it. He had the strength of three men. He was big and forebodin'."

"What did he look like?" asked Euan, cocking his head.

"He was very tall and had lots of muscles. His hair was long and light brown with a golden hue."

"Sounds like the Highland Storm," said one of the other men. "I'm surprised their laird can still fight so well since he's past his prime."

"Nay, this was a young man," she told him. "I dinna believe it was their laird. He travels with a red tail hawk that helped him fight by clawin' at the men's heads."

"A hawk? Damn, that must be Storm MacKeefe's son, called Hawke," said Euan. "He's twice the warrior of his faither."

"Let's get him," commanded Lennox, reaching for his weapon.

"There are eight of us and one of him. Surely, he canna kill us all," said one of the other clan members.

"Nay, please, dinna go," begged Phoebe, already so upset by

what she saw, and not wanting to lose any more men. "Take me back to the Highlands. Let my faither handle this."

"Our laird canna rule or make decisions in his condition. Plus, we're goin' back with four less men than we came with," Euan reminded her. "I think we need to even the score a little before we go."

"I beg ye, dinna do it." Phoebe couldn't forget the horrible sight of seeing her clansmen killed right before her very eyes. "The MacKeefe is a ruthless warrior. We canna lose any more men. Please, take me back to Crookston Castle and let my faither tend to this silly feud between the clans."

"It's no' silly," said Lennox. "The MacKeefes are responsible for the death of yer cousin, or have ye forgotten, lass?"

"Nay, I havena," she told them, missing her dear cousin, Osla, who was at one time like an older sister to her and also her best friend. Her father had told her many times while growing up that the MacKeefes were their sworn enemies. Phoebe often wished for her mother to console her, but her mother passed away when Phoebe was twelve. Even though she was only twelve years old, Phoebe ended up stepping in as Lady of the Castle.

When it seemed like the men weren't going to abide by her wish, she decided she needed to be firm. "I command ye to take me back to my faither. And if ye dinna do it, and somethin' happens to me, my faither will have all yer heads."

"Mayhap she's right," mumbled one of the men.

"She is Laird MacNab's favorite child," said Lennox. "I dinna want to be the one to have to tell him she is dead."

"No one's dyin'," snapped Euan. "We'll go back to collect the bodies and then head back home."

"Nay, we need to bury them here," protested Phoebe. "In this heat, their bodies will start smellin' before we get far. It'll take a full day or longer to get back to MacNab territory. If we are attacked along the way, it'll only slow us down to be haulin' dead weight."

Euan and Lennox spoke in hushed voices with their backs toward her. Then, looking over their shoulders, they discussed their plans while eyeing her. Finally, Euan turned around and nodded. "We'll bury the dead and head back home," he announced.

It was too easy. Phoebe's gut told her not to believe him, but she didn't have a choice. She was in their care and needed them to get her home safe and alive. There would be no traveling without them.

"Let's go," she told them, mounting her horse. "I'll show ye where the bodies are." As she sped away on her horse, she hoped they wouldn't meet up with the son of the Highland Storm again, because the man was terrifying, even though nothing usually scared her.

* * *

"HAWKE, I'll have a word with ye," called out Ian MacKeefe as he stormed across the practice field with Storm and Caleb following. Ian was a proud and strict man, having lost touch with Storm for years when they'd had a disagreement. He once had a hate for Sassenachs, but when he was reunited with his first English wife, Storm's mother, that all changed.

"It looks like yer grandda is no' happy about somethin'," said Logan, not that any of them doubted what this was all about.

"It's nothin' new," said Hawke. "Help me lift the caber."

Logan and Ethan helped to stand the caber up straight and Hawke hunkered down, hugging the end and lifting it in the air.

"Hawke, we need to talk to ye," called out Storm.

"Go ahead, Da," said Hawke, looking up at the end of the tall caber as he took two steps backward to steady himself, and then two forward before he flipped the pole end over end.

"Och, that's no' bad," said Storm, with a look of surprise upon his face. "Almost as guid as me, but not quite."

"I'm goin' to be the champion of the caber toss at the Highland Feis this year," Hawke told him, brushing his hands together to get rid of the dust.

"What did ye say?" asked Bridget as she and her father hurried after the group. "Did I hear ye are the champion of the caber toss?"

"Nay, no' him. I hold that title," said Storm proudly.

"Aye, but that is goin' to change this year," Hawke told them with confidence.

"Enough of the clishmaclaver," snorted Ian, throwing his hands in the air. "Grandson, Caleb tells us ye killed off four MacNabs on yer huntin' trip today. Is this true?"

Storm and Ian stood with their hands on their hips and scowls darkening their faces.

Hawke looked over to Caleb who quickly directed his gaze in the opposite direction. Hawke was planning on telling them about the attack, but was waiting until he had a chance to tell his father without a crowd of people and the chronicler around him.

"Dinna fash yerself," said Hawke, straightening his green and purple clan plaid as he spoke. "The MacNabs attacked me, and I took care of the situation, that's all."

"Ye fool!" spat Ian. "We have been tryin' to make amends with the MacNabs, no' cause a bigger rift between us."

"But the MacNabs have been feudin' with us ever since I can remember," Logan told them.

"Aye, but we had plans for an alliance," Storm told them. "It was almost settled that one of the MacKeefes would be betrothed to the chieftain's daughter."

"Humph," snorted Hawke. "Ye tried an alliance ten years ago and it didna work. I pity the poor man who has to marry the lass."

"It was supposed to have been ye," Storm told him, causing Hawke's head to snap up in surprise.

"Me?" he asked, making a face. "Nay. I dinna want to marry a

MacNab ever again. Nay, I tell ye. I dinna want anythin' to do with them."

"Ye're too auld no' to be married," his father told him in a low voice. It's gettin' to be an embarrassment, Hawke. Every time I try to find ye a lass to wed, ye turn her down.

"I willna go through that again." When Hawke was only eight and ten years of age, he'd married a girl from the MacNab Clan and it was the worst seven months of his life. The woman ended up dying and because of him, the feud with the MacNabs started up again. Usually, the MacKeefes weren't a warring clan, but sometimes the pride of Highlanders got in the way and only caused problems.

"What happened today?" asked Ian. "Why did ye kill them?"

"Why?" Hawke shook his head. "I told ye, four of them attacked me in the woods. I killed them in self-defense."

Ian and Storm exchanged glances. "Son, we ken ye are sometimes a hothead," said Hawke's father. "Mayhap ye thought they were attackin' but they really came in peace."

"Peace? A MacNab? And with swords drawn?" Hawke shook his head in disbelief. "Listen to yerself, Da. Ye canna really believe that. I might be a hothead at times, but I am no' daft. They attacked me, I tell ye."

"Well, did anyone else see the attack?" asked Ian.

"Nay," Caleb answered for him. "The three of us were off huntin' in another part of the forest." He motioned to his friends. "Hawke killed the four men all by himself."

"So no one was there to witness that it was an attack?" Storm raised a brow.

"Da, are ye sayin' ye dinna believe me?" Hawke was ready to scream. He felt insulted that his own father and grandfather didn't believe his words.

"We heard the cry of his hawk and came right away," said Logan, trying to help him.

"Aye," added Ethan. "But when we got there, all we saw were

four dead bodies and a bluidy sword in Hawke's hand. Hawke did it all by himself, and a guid thing, too, or he'd be dead. Right Hawke?"

"Stop tryin' to help," grumbled Hawke. His friends had good intentions, but were only making matters worse.

"Ye really killed four men all by yerself?" asked Brigham, leaning in and turning his ear toward them as if he didn't want to miss a word of this.

"Aye," Hawke said with a small nod.

"That sounds like somethin' that should go in the Highland Chronicles," said the man.

Hawke wanted to be mentioned in the book, but not this way. He wanted to be known for a heroic deed, not one that involved killing in self-defense. "Nay, 'twas nothin'," he said. "Besides, my da has taken down six men by himself in his days."

"We need to show respect for our enemies," said Storm. "Did they take their dead with them, Son?"

"I dinna think so," said Hawke. "There was only one left alive. He was a small man and I let him go."

"Ye did?" asked Bridget curiously. "Is that a normal course of action with attackers?"

"He wanted the survivor to give the message to the rest of the clan that they canna beat the MacKeefes," said Caleb, making Hawke want to box his ears.

"Did I teach ye nothin', Hawke?" asked Storm. "If ye let one go, there'll be ten more on yer doorstep come mornin'."

"So, then ye're sayin' I should have killed them all?" Hawke waited as his father contradicted himself.

"I'm sayin' ye shouldna have killed any of them," Storm answered. "Now, it is up to ye to go back and bury the bodies of the men ye killed."

"I'll help," offered Logan. "I'd like to pick up a new sword." He ran his hand over the hilt of his sword in thought.

"What about their horses?" asked Ethan eagerly. "I get first pick of those."

"Listen to ye bluidy warmongers," snapped Hawke's grandfather. "Nay, ye two will stay here and I'll take my grandson and a few men to do the job."

"I dinna need help," spat Hawke.

"I am no' comin' to help," answered Ian. "I'm only ridin' with ye to witness yer every move."

CHAPTER 4

As they approached the dead bodies, Phoebe felt an overpowering sadness engulf her. These were men she'd known from her clan. They had families back at Crookston Castle. Why did they have to attack one lone MacKeefe? If their vengeance hadn't consumed them, they'd still be alive right now.

They must have seen the MacKeefe man as an easy mark, not knowing what price they'd pay by their decisions. Then again, it was her who asked them to venture dangerously into MacKeefe territory because this was one of the only places where mugwort grew. She had wanted so badly to find it, but now it didn't seem that important anymore.

"Get the bodies buried quickly," ordered Euan. "And keep yer eyes open. If ye so much as see the plaid of the MacKeefes, attack, and dinna leave a one of them alive."

"Nay, what are ye sayin'?" asked Phoebe. "Havena enough men already died today?"

She waited as they buried the poor departed souls, all the while feeling a knot in her stomach. There were no MacKeefes here so she shouldn't feel so apprehensive. She supposed it was only because of what happened here earlier that made her feel uneasy.

The cry of a bird from above their heads had her looking up to the sky. "It's his hawk. The MacKeefe is comin'," she exclaimed.

"Guid." Euan unsheathed his sword. "Just what I'd hoped for."

"What are ye doin'?" Phoebe watched in horror as the men readied their weapons. "Our dead are buried," she told them. "Please, let's leave now and go back to Crookston Castle."

"No' before we have a chance to even the score," said Euan with a chuckle. "Men, hide behind the trees. We'll take him down before he even sees us comin'."

* * *

If Hawke hadn't been so upset that his own grandfather thought he was reckless and possibly lying to him, he would have heard Apollo's warning from the sky that there was trouble awaiting them.

"The attack happened just up ahead," explained Hawke, leading his grandfather and four of their clan members to the spot where he'd slain the MacNabs in self-defense.

"Where?" asked one of the men. "I dinna see any dead bodies."

"They're right up here," said Hawke, stopping his horse and looking around, thinking at first he'd made a mistake about the location. "They were here," he mumbled, his hand going to the hilt of his sword, expecting trouble. Before he could warn the others, they were attacked from the forest. A half-dozen MacNabs rode out with their weapons held high, catching the MacKeefes off guard.

"Get the big one first," yelled a man who seemed to be their leader.

One of the men threw a dagger. It whizzed past, almost hitting Hawke as he jerked back out of the way. With the one quick yank of the reins, the horse became skittish and reared up.

Caught off guard and losing his balance, Hawke tried to steady the horse but was thrown to the ground. His sword fell from his hand. When he reached for it, three men on horseback charged toward him. Hawke sprang to his feet, swiping at his attackers, managing to bring them to the ground. As he fought, three to one, Hawke became distracted by a woman's voice.

"He's the one. He's the man I saw kill our men," she shouted.

Hawke glanced up to see a woman standing at the edge of the forest. Her hood fell back, and dark black tresses spilled past her shoulders as she lifted her face to peruse him. It distracted him and, in that split second, he felt the sharp tip of a sword sink into his shoulder just below his collarbone. He involuntarily doubled over, only managing to get kicked next as the man removed the sword from his flesh. Stumbling backward, Hawke hit the ground hard, knocking his head against a rock.

"I killed the brute," shouted a man triumphantly. "Let's take care of the rest of them and get the hell out of here. Be sure to take their weapons and horses."

"Phoebe, hurry and go through the pockets of the dead and take everythin' ye can from the wretched curs," said another of the MacNabs.

Hawke's eyes drifted open slightly as his world spun before him. The pain in his shoulder hurt like the devil and he tasted bile rising to his throat. Through his blurred vision, he saw the MacNabs capturing his grandfather. All of the rest of the men who had come with Hawke from Hermitage Castle were slain, lying in puddles of blood.

"Nay," he mumbled, willing himself to move, but he couldn't. He was no longer sure he wouldn't die with the rest of them. The sound of horses' hooves on the hard earth echoed in his ears as the MacNabs retreated into the forest.

"Let me go," he heard Ian MacKeefe shouting. "I hate ye all. Ye just killed my grandson! I'll have yer bluidy heads for it. I will have my revenge!"

"The way I see it, we're even now," came a MacNab's reply. "Yer grandson is to blame for all this. He killed four of our men earlier and now four of yers are dead in exchange."

"My son, Storm, willna let ye get away with this," warned Ian. "He'll hunt ye down like dogs. He's the Highland Storm."

The man chuckled. "Well, I hope he's better with a sword than yer grandson. After all, he couldna seem to save ye. Now, we'll hold ye for ransom and take everythin' from the bluidy MacKeefes, Hermitage Castle included."

Through slitted eyes, Hawke saw his bird up in the sky. Apollo flew in circles above them, shrieking.

"I wish we had an arrow to shut that bird up," snarled one of the other men.

"Phoebe, let's go," someone called out. "Yer faither is goin' to be happy we brought him The MacKeefe."

"Aye, we'll be in the laird's favors now, especially after losin' four men," said another.

"I have one more man to check," the woman answered, her voice coming closer to Hawke. He heard her light footsteps and the sweep of her gown over the dry earth as she approached him.

Then Hawke felt the light touch of a woman's hand going through his pockets. It took all his strength to keep from drifting into an unconscious state since his pain was so intense. The MacNabs had stolen his sword but he still had a dagger hidden in the waistband of his plaid. Hawke had to do something to save his grandfather or die trying. He would not lose him and neither would he return to the castle without him. Suddenly, an idea came to him. This would be his only chance, so he needed to stay conscious to do it.

His hand lashed out and gripped the girl's wrist as his eyes popped open, scaring her since she thought he was dead.

"Och!" she cried, looking down at Hawke in terror. Fear filled her hazel eyes. Because she was startled, it gave him the advantage. She was just a wench so it should be easy to hold her, even with his wounds and his pounding head. Stirring up the strength he needed to continue with his plan, Hawke pulled her to him. At the same time, he sat up, trying to concentrate so he wouldn't pass out.

With his free hand, he reached for his hidden dagger. Then he got to his feet, pulling the wench toward him, holding his blade to her throat.

"Release Ian MacKeefe or I'll kill her, I swear I will!" he shouted, stopping the MacNabs from leaving. Blood covered his chest from his wound, soaking into the girl's clothes as well. Her body trembled beneath his touch, but she did not fight him.

"He's no' dead, ye fools!" cried the man in charge.

"Euan, I'm sorry. I could have sworn he was," answered a man from their clan. "I had a hard time removin' my sword from his flesh."

"I should kill ye, Lennox for bein' so daft."

"Release him," Hawke called out, keeping his blade to the girl's throat.

"Hawke, what are ye doin'?" shouted Ian. His hands were tied behind his back and he was thrown face down over one of the horses.

"Release him, Euan," shouted the girl. "Do what he says. My life is at stake."

"Nay," answered the man stubbornly, turning a half-circle on his horse. "We're takin' The MacKeefe back to our laird." He looked over at Hawke and only hesitated for a moment before he continued. "Keep the girl. I dinna care."

"What?" both Hawke and the girl said at the same time.

"We dinna need her," continued Euan, raising his arm in the air, signaling to the others. "Let's go, men."

"But Euan, Laird Angus is goin' to kill us if we let anythin' happen to his daughter," said the man named Lennox.

"Haud yer wheesht, ye cur!" spat Euan. "I'm the one givin' the orders. We'll bring The MacKeefe back to Crookston Castle and then decide what to do. We've got ourselves a fortune here. He's worth more than the wench and will get us what we want."

"A trade. Let's do a trade right here, right now," Hawke offered, not believing they would leave one of their own women there, especially the daughter of their laird. What kind of men were they? Hawke would risk his life to protect any of the women of their clan.

"Nay, no trade," answered the man stubbornly. "Men, we are leavin'. Now!"

"We're goin' to leave Phoebe here with the enemy?" asked one of the MacNabs.

"He willna hurt her," spat Euan.

"How can ye be sure?" asked Lennox.

"Because," said Euan, holding his dagger in the air. "If he harms a hair on Phoebe's head, their chieftain dies. Now, let's move on out."

With that, the leader of the MacNabs left with Hawke's grandfather slung over a horse like naught more than bagged game.

"Damn it," Hawke spat, looking up at Apollo, closing one eye in the bright sun. The bird landed in a tree nearby. "Now ye come to help me," he complained. "A little late, dinna ye think?" Hawke scanned the dead bodies of four of his clan members, feeling his heart about ready to burst in his chest from grief. Wasted lives, and all for naught. These men shouldn't have died today. And his grandfather never should have been taken prisoner. Hawke should have been able to stop it from happening, and possibly could have if he hadn't been distracted by the girl.

"Let's go," he told her, pushing her toward her horse hidden in the forest. He wasn't looking forward to returning to Hermitage Castle and telling his father that Ian MacKeefe was captured and four of their men were dead. Neither did he want to admit that he'd been attacked by the MacNabs for the second time that day.

CHAPTER 5

"Let me go!" cried Phoebe, struggling against the man's hold. He sat on the horse behind her, holding one arm tightly around her waist and his other hand gripping the reins.

"Nay," he growled in her ear. "Ye are the only hope I have of gettin' my grandda back alive."

"Yer grandfaither is the laird of the MacKeefe Clan?" she asked.

"He and my da both. They share the title since we hold lands in the Highlands as well as Hermitage Castle in the Lowlands."

"So that makes ye just as valuable as me."

"I doubt that," he said, squinting one eye and looking up to the sky. His head spun and he couldn't see straight. He'd never make it back to Hermitage Castle in this condition. There was a creek up ahead. If he could just wrap his wound and get a drink of water, perhaps he'd be able to ride back to the castle. He directed the horse deeper into the forest.

"Where are ye takin' me?" she asked.

"We're goin' to stop at the water's edge. My wound needs tendin' to and ye are goin' to do it."

"Nay, I willna!"

"Ye'll do as I say."

"Ye canna make me." She turned her head slightly and glared at him, as if he were some kind of monster. The wench tried his patience.

"I'm the one holdin' the blade unless ye've forgotten." He stopped at the creek and, with great effort, slid from the horse. When he did, the girl jumped off and started running in the opposite direction.

"I dinna have the time for this," Hawke said, whistling and calling his hawk down from the sky.

Apollo chased after the girl, flying just above her head. Its wingspan alone was almost as long as the girl was tall. It left her in shadow as they moved. She screamed and dropped to the ground using her arms to cover her head. "Nay! Call off yer bird and stop this."

Hawke chuckled. "If ye try to run again, I'll command my bird to hunt ye down."

"Nay, dinna do that," she begged. "I already saw what it did to one of my clan members."

"Then get back here and dress my wound."

"Aye," she answered. "But please, call off yer bird."

"Apollo, come." Hawke held out his arm, clad in leather. It was his left arm that was affected by his wound. The bird landed, using his arm as a perch. The red tail hawk was quite large. Since Hawke was wounded, it felt twice as heavy in his weakened state. He put the bird atop the horse's pommel so the girl wouldn't think of trying to steal his steed and ride away next.

Dropping to his knees at the edge of the water, Hawke moaned as he splashed cold water on his face. When he looked down, he saw his reflection in the ripples and the water was red from his blood. He fell back to a sitting position, holding his hand over the gash, letting out a deep breath, closing his eyes. Thankfully, the leather covering his shoulder and arm that he wore under his tunic for the bird to perch on had helped to slow down the bleeding.

"Let me have a look at that," came a soft voice from next to him.

He opened his eyes to see the MacNab girl staring at his shoulder. Using one hand and his teeth, Hawke pulled at his leine, ripping the cloth from his body. He then handed it to her, leaving him bare-chested "Here," he told her. "Rip this into strips and wrap it around my wound to stop the bleedin'."

"Nay," she said, getting up and walking over to the horse.

"Dinna give me trouble," he warned her without turning around. "I might have to call for Apollo to come after ye again, and it could be deadly." His bird had never killed a human, only small game and fowl, but she didn't need to know that. Apollo was able to claw at a man and cause considerable damage.

"Ye dinna have to threaten me. I'm only gettin' my herbs for yer wound. If ye dinna cleanse and treat it properly, ye might die."

"I'm surprised that ye almost sound as if ye care."

There was a moment of silence, the sound of the rushing water the only noise between them. Sun beat down upon Hawke's head and tall grass swayed in the summer breeze. The smell of wildflowers filled his senses. This all might have seemed peaceful if it were in a different situation.

"I am a healer, MacKeefe," came the girl's words as she approached him. "It is no' in my nature to walk away from one in need."

"Hawke," he told her.

She settled her things next to him and looked back at the bird on the horse. "Aye. It's a red tailed hawk, if I'm no' mistaken."

"Nay. Me. My name is Hawke."

"Oh." She wet a cloth in the stream and cleansed his wound. He winced at the sting of the cold water biting at his severed flesh as she dabbed at his wound. "I am Phoebe MacNab," she told him.

"I ken."

Her hand stilled as if she were being cautious. "Ye do?"

"I heard yer clansmen call ye Phoebe," he said, looking up at her from the corners of his eyes as she worked.

"I see."

FOR SOME REASON, when Phoebe heard her name on the MacKeefe's tongue, it sent a shiver up her spine. Hawke was a dangerous man. She knew that by seeing the way he fought. If he weren't wounded right now, she might be frightened of being so close to him. But he was vulnerable in this situation and had also lost a lot of blood. She would use this to her advantage.

Phoebe continued to tend to his wound, not liking the fact she was helping the enemy, but still, she couldn't just let the man die. She was angrier right now with Euan and Lennox for leaving her behind. Hopefully, her father would punish them severely when he found out. But in her father's condition, she wasn't sure he could make a decision, lead an army, or even get out of bed right now.

"The wound looks deep and needs stitchin'," she told him. "I canna tell how much damage has been done because there is too much bluid. However, this leather ye wear beneath yer leine stopped the blade from hittin' a bone or damagin' a muscle as far as I can tell. However, I'm goin' to have to remove it."

"Just wrap the wound and I'll have the healer tend to it when we get to Hermitage Castle," he instructed.

"No need to wait. Ye might bleed to death by then. I have a needle and thread in my travel bag." She made her way back to the horse, pausing when she noticed the hawk's eyes flash toward her. But then the hawk lifted its head and flew up into the sky to chase a bird. She could have taken that moment to hop on the horse and try to escape, but something inside wouldn't let her go. This man needed her help. Being a healer, she couldn't turn her back on him even if he was her enemy.

"Why did yer people attack me? Twice?" asked Hawke as Phoebe removed the leather from his body. Then she wet the end of the thread between her lips and pushed the thread through the eye of the needle.

"I dinna ken. I urged them no' to, but Euan is reckless."

"Reckless," he repeated, making a face and shaking his head as if the word meant something to him. "Four of my men died for naught today. And now I have to go back to the clan and tell their families the bad news."

"What about the four men who died from my clan?" she asked him, sticking the needle through his skin. He winced and clenched his jaw.

"They attacked me. I was only defendin' myself," he told her, reaching for something in his sporran.

"What are ye doin'?" she asked.

"I need somethin' for the pain."

"That's what the herbs are for," she told him. "I'll apply them once the wound is closed."

"Nay, that's no' what I mean." He reached into his boot and pulled out a small metal flask. Unscrewing the top, he held the vessel up to his mouth and swallowed down some liquid, letting out a sigh of satisfaction.

"Whisky?" she asked, recognizing the smell. Gingerly, she pulled the thread through his skin.

"Mountain Magic," he said, through gritted teeth, raising the flask and taking another swig. He swallowed forcefully which told her he felt the pain from her ministrations.

"Mountain Magic? What's that?" she asked.

"Ye dinna ken?" He acted as if she should know. "My great-granddda makes it. It is what keeps him alive this long."

"I'd like some as well," she told him, knotting the thread and breaking it with her teeth.

"Nay. This is no' for lassies. It is very strong."

"Give it to me," she said, snatching it from his hand, not liking when someone told her she couldn't do something. It only made her want to prove them wrong. She'd tasted strong whisky before, so this was nothing new. Lifting the flask to her lips, he stopped her with his words.

"I'm warnin' ye lass . . . dinna do it."

She cocked a smile, staring him straight in the eyes as she took a big swallow . . . and almost died! It felt like the fires of hell burning a path down her throat. Phoebe wasn't at all sure that her body wasn't on fire. Her hand shot up around her neck. She couldn't breathe!

"Are ye all right?" he asked. "Yer face is turnin' blue."

She tried to inhale but couldn't. The whisky was so potent that it was sure to kill her. She wheezed in an attempt to get some air.

His head jerked upward and concern painted his face. "Ye really canna breathe, can ye?"

Phoebe shook her head, reaching out one hand for him, silently begging for his help. She didn't want to die this way.

"By the rood, ye are no' jestin'!" Hawke jumped up and pulled her into his arms, hitting her over and over on the back. It did nothing to help. It only aggravated her because it hurt. He was a big man and stronger than he knew. She held her palms against his chest, feeling as if she were going to pass out.

Then the fool did something she never expected. He pressed his lips up against hers in a kiss! What was he doing? She was dying and couldn't breathe, and all he could think about was lust? Then she quickly changed her opinion of him when she felt him blowing the breath of life into her mouth. It cleared her airway and she gasped, pulling away, coughing and choking.

"Guid," he said.

"Guid?" she asked, still coughing. "I am dyin' and ye say guid?"

"If ye are coughin' and talkin' then ye arena dyin', lass. I did the only thing I could to give ye air."

"Och. I see," she said, feeling suddenly foolish. This man, her enemy, just saved her life. "Why did ye help me?" she asked softly, needing to know.

"Ye are doin' the same for me, so I thought it was only fair."

"But ye commanded me to help ye. Ye didna have to do anythin' to stop me from dyin'. We're enemies"

"I suppose ye're right." He shrugged and winced when he moved his hurt shoulder. "But I canna stand by and watch a bonnie lassie in need without doin' somethin' about it. Even if she is my enemy." He sat down on a rock and let out another moan.

"Bonnie?" She peeked out from the corners of her eyes as she stood over him and applied an herbal ointment to his wound. His head turned and their gazes met. The connection between them made her momentarily forget that she was staring into the face of a cold-hearted killer. There, in the depths of his beautiful, bright blue eyes, she saw concern and kindness, not hatred and revenge at all.

"Aye, lass. Ye are very bonnie," he whispered, reaching up gently to caress a lock of her hair. Then his gaze traveled over to her mouth. He leaned forward, pulling her closer, and brought his lips to meet hers once again.

Phoebe hesitated and her body stiffened. He must have seen her uncertainty because of what he said next.

"Close yer eyes, lass. Forget for a moment that we are enemies. Instead, try to pretend that I am yer lover."

She should have walked away at hearing that, or perhaps slapped him for such a vulgar, brash suggestion. But she didn't. Something about this man and the situation made her stay.

Standing there, she waited for what would happen next. Her eyes closed as he gently cradled her chin with his large hand, bringing his mouth to hers. But this time, he wasn't blowing air into her lungs and it had naught to do with saving her life. This was a kiss a man would give his lover. It was filled with passion! She liked it. It made her go weak in the knees, and she prayed that she wouldn't fall at his feet. Never had she been kissed by a man this way. Actually, she'd never even been kissed by a man at all. Just one touch of his soft lips to hers and it seemed as if she could feel all his emotions running through her at once. While it excited her, it also scared her out of her mind.

Hawke was a big, rugged Highlander who feared nothing. He could force himself on her right there in the woods, or even snap her neck with one huge hand if he wanted to. Suddenly, she felt scared.

Her eyes popped open and she jerked back, trying to make distance between them.

"What's the matter, Phoebe? Not used to kissin' yer enemy?" he asked with a slight chuckle.

Mayhap it was the word enemy that brought her back to her senses, making her remember just who he was.

"We are no' friends and neither are we alliances, so I warn ye no' to do that again!"

"Aye, we are enemies," he said with a nod. "Still, ye have to admit that ye liked it." He studied her face as if he were looking straight into her soul, and it seemed as if he knew all her secrets. It wouldn't do any good to lie because she was sure he knew the truth. She did like it. A little too much. The kiss made her feel alive and this scared her even more. No one had ever made her feel this way before.

Feeling tired, hot, hungry and confused, she didn't know what to think anymore. Hawke muddled her mind and that wasn't good. She would have to be careful around him. This could all be naught but a ploy to get what he wanted. And whatever a man like Hawke MacKeefe wanted, she was sure she was not willing to give.

She busied herself ripping apart his leine. Then, using a length of cloth to bind his wound, she wrapped it under one of his arms and around his back, tying a mean knot at his chest.

"No' so hard," he said with a grunt, making her realize she'd hurt him. Funny that she could make a hardened warrior flinch. She liked having that power over him. It gave her the confidence she needed that mayhap she could escape after all.

"It's done," she said, gathering up her herbs and ointments.

"Already?" He sounded disappointed if she wasn't mistaken. "Mayhap ye should check the stitches," he suggested, reaching for the bandage.

"Nay!" With a slap of her hand against his, she stopped him. "Do no' touch the wound. It needs to heal." She made her way to the horse with the supplies.

Hawke got to his feet, rubbing his slapped hand and looking like a child who had been scolded. "I thought ye liked the kiss, lass."

"Nay. I didna," she lied, putting her things into the travel bag tied to the horse, being sure not to look at him when she said it. If so, he'd know the truth.

"My mistake," he said, leather creaking from the saddle as he pulling his large body up atop the horse. Leaning over, and with his good arm, he reached down for her.

Phoebe closed the bag and latched it, her eyes slowly traveling up his proffered arm. Without his leine, it was easier for her to see each muscle and ripple of his bronzed, wide chest that told her he was a strong warrior. It also reminded her that she was at his mercy. His long hair lifted around his shoulders in the breeze as his blue eyes drank her in. As rugged as he was, he was still very handsome. Much handsomer than he was when she first saw him ten years ago when she was only a child.

Memories swept through her, making her miss her cousin, Osla, who had been married to Hawke before she died by his hand. Questions in her mind rose to the surface, telling her she needed to keep her distance from this dangerous man. Still, for some reason, it was difficult for her to look away. She kept thinking about the kiss they'd just shared and how gentle he'd been with her. It was so unlike the touch of a murderer, or so she guessed. That tenderness they'd shared between them led her mind to wondering about doing other things with this MacKeefe man as well.

"Nay," she said, shaking her head to clear it of her disgusting lustful daydreams. She had to remember he was the enemy and also responsible for Osla's death. She shouldn't be having these kinds of feelings for a man like him. What was the matter with her?

"Nay?" he asked in confusion, pulling back his hand. "All right, then climb into the saddle yerself if ye must. I was only tryin' to assist ye."

She didn't realize she'd said the word aloud. It wasn't meant to reject his proffered hand, but rather to dismiss the ill thoughts from her head. But now that he'd heard her, she couldn't admit the real reason and what she'd been thinking. So, instead, she reached out, putting one foot in the stirrup and pulling herself up.

Phoebe never had trouble mounting her horse by herself, but this was different. Now a big warrior was seated in the saddle, taking up every bit of room. She wasn't sure what to do with her leg. Not being able to lift it over him, she teetered in the air and started to fall backward.

"Whoa there, lass," he said, clamping his hands around her waist and dragging her atop his lap. Without thinking, she wrapped her arms around his neck to keep from falling.

"Now, isna this cozy?" he asked, with a half-grin and a slight chuckle. The nerve of him to jest after what she'd been through today.

Angrily, she hiked up her skirt and lifted one leg over to the other side of the horse. As she slid down in front of him, he moved backward to give her more room. Being a Scot, Phoebe always sat astride atop her horse, instead of sidesaddle. If she were an English lady, mayhap she would have used a lady's saddle instead. But in the rugged hills of Scotland, there was no such thing as proper.

"My faither is goin' to be furious when he finds out ye abducted me."

"Really?" he asked, nonchalantly, poking at his wound. "It doesna seem as if yer clansmen think so, or they never would have left ye behind."

The truth upset her and made her even madder. "Well, they made a bad decision and they'll pay for it. I'll make sure of it. Right after I return to Crookston Castle."

"I'll say they made a bad decision," he agreed. "And when my da finds out they've taken my grandda captive, the feud will turn into a bigger battle between our clans than it was a decade ago."

"And what will happen to ye when ye get back to the castle and tell yer da that ye werena able to save the lives of yer men, nor keep the MacNabs from abductin' yer chieftain?" she asked with a smug smile.

"Dinna fash yerself," he grumbled. "I'll take care of that."

It was clear to Phoebe that this thought troubled Hawke and he was trying not to show it. She could hear in his tone that his confidence was suddenly shaken. This might work well to her advantage. She hoped so. Because, if not, she didn't know what she was going to do. It was imperative that she get back home right away to help her ailing father. Nay, she could not be a prisoner of the MacKeefes, no matter what.

CHAPTER 6

Logan, Caleb, and Ethan ran to meet Hawke as soon as he rode through the gate of Hermitage Castle. Feeling sick to his stomach after everything that had transpired, Hawke dreaded having to make the announcement that couldn't be avoided.

"Where are the other men?" asked Caleb, looking behind him down the drawbridge.

"Aye, where is our chieftain?" asked Logan in confusion.

"And who is she?" Ethan pointed at the girl sitting in front of Hawke.

Hawke slowly lowered himself from the horse, reaching back up to help Phoebe dismount.

"Ye're wounded," said Ethan, noticing the blood on Hawke and the bandage. "What happened?"

Hawke's father, as well as his grandmother, Lady Clarista, ran across the courtyard to meet them. They were followed by the rest of the clan.

"Hawke, you're hurt," said his English grandmother, reaching out to gently touch him on the arm. "Where is my husband? I hope he's not hurt, too. With his age, he doesn't heal fast anymore." She looked around and frowned.

"Son, I think ye better tell us what happened," said Storm in a low voice.

"We were attacked by the MacNabs," said Hawke with a deep sigh. "I'm sorry to say that four of our men are dead and our enemy has taken Ian with them."

Several wails went up from the wives of the deceased at hearing the awful news. The women pulled their children close to them for comfort. It stabbed at Hawke's heart to see not only the crying widows, but also the frightened looks in the children's eyes. He wanted to comfort each one of them personally, but couldn't do that right now.

"Was Ian wounded?" asked Clarista, keeping her chin high, staying strong as she pulled one of the women of the dead men to her and rubbed her back to comfort her.

"Nay," Hawke answered with a shake of his head. Sweat beaded on his brow. "Grandda was not harmed as far as I ken."

"Where did they take him?" asked Storm.

"I believe they took him back to their castle and will be demandin' a ransom soon."

"Well, where the hell were ye when this was all goin' on?" Storm ran a troubled hand through his hair and his jaw clenched tightly. "God's eyes, Hawke. Ye are one of my best warriors. I counted on ye to keep the others safe and now they're dead. And ye ken better than anyone that Ian is no' the man he used to be. Yer grandfaither might no' come out of this alive if they decide to torture him."

"I'm sorry, Da," Hawke apologized meekly, his hand going to his wound. "I ken I should have been able to save them. I didna mean to let everyone down."

PHOEBE COULDN'T BELIEVE that Hawke was taking the blame for

something that was out of his control. His clan seemed to hold him responsible for what happened, saying he should have protected the others and kept the laird from being taken. There was nothing he could have done. He was wounded and left for dead. Nay, it truly wasn't his fault. Still, Hawke said nothing in his defense. Phoebe didn't like it. The man needed to speak up and defend himself. If he wouldn't do it, she decided that she would tell them the truth about what happened.

"Hawke was stabbed, kicked, beaten, thrown from a horse, and left for dead," said Phoebe. "I stitched his wound, but he has lost a lot of bluid and needs to rest."

Everyone looked at her in shock for speaking so brashly. The crowd became quiet. Finally, Storm spoke.

"And who might ye be, lassie?"

"I'm Phoebe," she told him. "Phoebe MacNab," she answered proudly, raising her chin in the air and looking directly at them. "My faither is Angus MacNab, our clan's chieftain."

"She's the enemy," someone shouted.

"How dare ye bring her inside our castle walls," cried someone else.

"Kill her," shouted a man from the back of the crowd.

Hawke noticed the king's chronicler and his daughter making their way to the front. What happened today wasn't something Hawke wanted listed in their writings.

"Wait," shouted Hawke, lifting his hand in the air, and wavering back and forth. "I didna tell ye all of it. When I was lyin' there, left for dead, Phoebe tried to pick my pocket."

"Then she's also a thief!" cried one woman.

"Hang her," shouted a man. "We canna trust any MacNab. Especially no' a woman."

"Haud yer wheesht! All of ye," commanded Storm. "I dinna want to hear another word about this before I've had a chance to talk to my son in private. Hawke, meet me in my solar anon."

"Aye, Da," said Hawke, looking over at Phoebe. "What about her?"

"Put her in the dungeon," said Storm.

Phoebe's eyes opened wide and shot over to Hawke. "Nay. Please. No' the dungeon," she begged.

"I canna take the chance that ye are goin' to escape," explained Storm.

HAWKE SHOULDN'T HAVE CARED what happened to the girl, but somehow he did. And when she looked at him with those terrified eyes, begging him not to put her in the dungeon, he couldn't bring himself to agree with his father. He had to protect her.

"Nay, Da. She's done nothin' wrong. No lassie should have to spend time in the dungeon. Ye should agree with that since ye always tell me Mathair was once imprisoned right here at Hermitage Castle and how awful it was."

"That's right, Da." Renard, Hawke's older brother by over ten years, stepped through the crowd. Renard was tall and lean and had red hair. He was raised as English, but now embraced the ways of the Scot and wore his plaid proudly. "Dinna ye remember how awful ye felt when Mathair was put in the dungeon? I remember bein' there with her when I was a boy. I have to admit, at the time it was terrifyin'. Mayhap Hawke is right. This girl is only a lass."

"All right then, I willna throw her in the dungeon," said Storm, scanning the faces of the angry crowd. "But Hawke, ye are responsible for her. She is our prisoner and it is important that ye keep a close eye on her and dinna let her escape. She is our only hope of getting Ian back alive."

"Let's go," said Hawke, putting his hand on Phoebe's back.

"Wait!" Lady Clarista stopped him. "She is covered in blood. Let me help her clean up and give her a change of clothes first. We'll meet ye in the great hall later."

"I am no' sure about this, Mathair," said Storm under his breath, his eyes flashing across the crowd eagerly as everyone waited for his reply.

"I'll be responsible for her as well," said Lady Clarista. "Mayhap that's no' a guid idea, Grandmathair," said Hawke. "She is a MacNab and no' to be trusted."

Phoebe spoke up. "I'm a MacNab surrounded by thick fortress walls and a courtyard filled with angry MacKeefes who all look like they want to lop off my head right now."

Hawke looked out at the crowd and realized she was right. Vengeance filled their eyes because of what happened today and he couldn't blame them. He wet his parched lips, knowing he had to say something. "If anyone even thinks of harmin' the lass, they'll have to deal with me."

"Come on, Son. Both of ye," said Storm, talking to Hawke and Renard. "Aidan, Ian and Onyx, I'd like ye to join us as well."

"We're here," said Aidan, rushing over.

"How about us?" asked Logan. "We're here to help, too. Let us join in the discussion with Hawke and our faithers."

"Fine," said Storm, throwing his hands in the air. "All of ye, follow me. And someone find Heartha to take a look at Hawke's wound."

"Storm, did you forget that Heartha is spending time at Blake Castle in Devonshire?" asked Clarista. "We don't have a healer right now."

"Blethers, I forgot about that." Storm looked across the courtyard, spying Orrick, the old sorcerer. "Orrick, bring yer bag of potions," shouted Storm. "And mayhap bring that crystal ball of yers or anythin' that can aid us in bringin' home my faither."

"Storm?" Orrick hurried over to join them. The man didn't look any different than the first time Hawke met him when Hawke was a child. Everyone around him seemed to grow older, but Orrick stayed the same. "I don't have a crystal ball," Orrick told him. "But Zara, the gypsy, gave me some Tarot Cards. Did you want me to read those for you?"

"Nay! Anythin' but the Tarot," said Storm, holding up his hand to ward something away. "That brings back too many memories. Just bring your herbs and ointments."

"I can help Hawke," Phoebe spoke up. "I am a healer."

"Nay," answered Storm. "Ye are the enemy and would probably poison him."

"She was the one to stitch me up and bind my wound," Hawke explained to his father.

"Perhaps Phoebe and Orrick can both minister Hawke for his wound," suggested Clarista.

"Really?" Phoebe's eyes lit up and she no longer looked scared. "I would like that," she said, smiling at Orrick.

"Can she?" Clarista asked her son's permission.

"Do what ye want," grunted Storm, with a wave of his hand. "I dinna have time for this clishmaclaver. We need to make a plan to bring home faither."

"Let's go," Hawke told them, leading the way to the solar. "I think I ken a way to get grandda back, and I am goin' to be the one to do it."

* * *

HAWKE PLOPPED down atop the bed as soon as they entered the solar. He was broken, beaten, and totally exhausted. For some reason, he felt worse than when he returned from a battle. It weighed heavy on his mind that he wasn't able to stop today's attacks from happening.

"All right. Tell us everythin' that happened," said Aidan, turning a chair backward and straddling it, giving Hawke his undivided attention.

"And leave nothin' out," added Onyx. Onyx was raised as a MacKeefe, but found out later in life that he was really an English noble. His eyes were what made everyone think he was a demon, one being black and the other orange. He and his English wife, Lovelle, lived in England the majority of the time, but Onyx spent a lot of time in Scotland with his good friends, Aidan and Ian, who were like brothers to him. His son, Ethan, was the product of a youthful tryst.

"Caleb, open the window for some air," said Ian to his son, carrying a tankard of ale that he brought with him from the great hall. Ian's tall frame and dark hair made him look mysterious. His son, Caleb, inherited his dark looks but not the height. Hawke's grandfather's name was also Ian, but it was a common name amongst the Scots.

"Aye, Da," said Caleb, pulling open the shutter and letting in light and air. Sunshine streamed across Hawke's legs and the slight breeze felt good against his burning skin. He let out a breath and tried to relax.

"What happened, Hawke?" asked Storm with concern in his voice.

"We went to the attack site and the dead men were missin'," Hawke relayed the information.

"The MacNabs must have taken the bodies with them," said Renard.

"Nay." Hawke closed his eyes and laid his head back on the pillow, wanting to sleep. "When they attacked us, they didna have the bodies with them. They must have buried them instead."

"Didna ye realize the MacNabs were there?" asked Ian.

"No' at first," said Hawke. "I thought I'd killed all of them except for the one I let go."

"Ye did?" asked Aidan.

"Aye. It was actually the girl," said Hawke. "I didna ken she was a lass at the time. When I saw her standin' there durin' the second attack – I – I was distracted. And with three men comin' at me at once, I failed to hold them off."

"How many times do I need to tell ye no' to lose yer focus, Son?" asked Storm.

Hawke's eyes opened and he looked straight at his father. "Ye also told me no' to fight if I didna have to," Hawke reminded him. "Ye spent a lot of time in yer past winnin' yer earnin's in competitions rather than fightin', Da, if I must remind ye."

"He's right," agreed Onyx. "Ye did tell us that, Storm."

"It doesna matter." Storm paced the room. "What does matter is that we lost four guid men today and my faither is being held captive. What are we goin' to do to remedy that?"

"We'll attack the MacNabs and take Ian back," suggested Ethan.

"Aye," agreed Logan, resting his hand on the hilt of his sword. "We have plenty of men in the clan to fight back."

"Nay, that's too risky," said Caleb, not agreeing with his friends. "Crookston Castle is a strong fortress closer to our Highland camp than to our castle here on the border. Usin' Hermitage Castle for cover is out of the question since it is too far away. With only our camp in the Highlands, we'll be an easy mark."

"That's right," agreed Caleb's father. "We'd be at a disadvantage."

"Let's wait until they ask for a ransom," said Aidan, coming up with a solution. "Then we'll set up a spot to meet with them and lop off their heads." Aidan swiped his hand across his throat for effect.

"Nay, that willna work either," said Storm, continuing to pace. "They might retaliate and attack our camp in the Highlands. A lot of our clan's women and children are there right now. We need to make sure they're protected."

"Then bring them to the castle," said Ethan. "Or at least until our battle with the MacNabs is over."

"Nay," said Hawke. "We've been feudin' for as long as I can remember. This will never end. We need to find another way."

"There is no other way," said Renard. "We need to move in quickly."

"I have another plan that just might work," said Hawke with a yawn.

"What is that, Son?" asked Storm.

"I'll sneak into their castle, by myself, and break grandda out of the dungeon."

"Ye're addlepated!" spat Caleb. "Ye'll be killed before ye set a foot anywhere near the dungeon."

"I say we make an alliance, just like we were plannin' to do before this happened," said Storm.

"What kind of alliance?" asked Logan.

"Hawke will marry MacNab's daughter, Phoebe. Then, we'll go to the castle and demand they return Ian."

"Or what?" asked Hawke, throwing his hands in the air. "It'll never work. Phoebe's own clansmen left her behind, so I doubt she's of any value to them. Besides, I'm no' gettin' married to anyone right now."

"What if they willna release the prisoner even after the marriage?" asked Ethan. "Then what guid will that have done? We canna kill off Hawke's wife."

"That's right. I'm sure Hawke doesna want to lose two wives," said Logan.

Hawke grunted, not wanting to think about the last time he'd married for the sake of an alliance when everything went wrong. He was framed by the MacNabs for the death of Osla but couldn't prove it. Still, he felt responsible. If he hadn't left her alone during the hunt, she might still be alive today. He felt hesitant to put himself in the same situation again, but he had no choice. There was nothing else they could do to save his grandfather before the bloody MacNabs tortured him. The man was getting older and his health had been getting worse these past few years. Hawke couldn't let him die without trying to save him.

"I'd rather no' talk about losin' wives," said Hawke, looking at his wound and touching it gently. He was still bleeding, even with his stitches.

"Hawke, ye need to rest," said Storm. "I'll send Orrick up to look at yer wound. Everyone else, meet me in the stable. We have four dead clan members to bring back and bury, and I willna let them lie there and rot while the ravens peck out their eyes."

"Aye," agreed the Madmen MacKeefe, heading for the door.

"What are we goin' to do about our chieftain?" asked Caleb, speaking of Hawke's grandfather.

Storm stopped pacing and stared out the window. "If we have to stay up all night devisin' a plan, then we'll do it. But, I swear I willna let the MacNabs best us, or take my faither's life."

CHAPTER 7

After washing up and changing her clothes, Phoebe ran a boar's bristle brush through her hair. A servant girl wrung out a rag in the basin of water across the room and Lady Clarista was next to the bed.

"Thank ye, Lady Clarista, for lendin' me one of yer gowns," said Phoebe. Hermitage Castle was a square fortress and much smaller than Crookston Castle. Still, it was a sturdy stronghold and well kept. The solar room she now occupied was Lady Clarista's. It was decorated in a grand manner with colorful, woven tapestries filling the walls. A large bed was raised up on a pedestal. The mattress looked thick and was covered with a burgundy blanket that was embroidered with small colorful flowers.

"I know it's a little too big for you, dear, but it's better than wearing a gown soaked in blood," answered Clarista, putting Phoebe's dirty clothes in a pile and handing them to the maidservant. Phoebe felt odd wearing the green, purple and brown plaid of the MacKeefes, but she had no other choice. She only hoped to don her own clan colors of red and black before she met up with the MacNabs again.

"I'm sorry about yer husband," said Phoebe, feeling bad for the woman that her husband was now a prisoner, the same as she.

Clarista raised her head and pushed back a gray lock of hair. "At least my husband is still alive, as far as we know. Some of the clanswomen were not so lucky today with the fate of their husbands. The widows are going to have a hard time raising their children on their own."

"I ken." Phoebe played with the brush, no longer able to look into Clarista's eyes. She felt really bad about what happened. "I tried to stop my clan from attackin' but they wouldna listen. If my faither had been here, things would have been different."

Clarista silently nodded to the maidservant, dismissing her. After the girl left the room with Phoebe's dirty clothes, Clarista closed the door and slowly turned around.

"It is all the horrible reality of war," she told Phoebe. "Every wife fears for the life of her husband every single day. No one wants to lose a loved one, let alone see their bloody, broken bodies lying at their feet."

A shiver ran through Phoebe as she thought of the MacNabs as well as the MacKeefes that she saw killed today. She, as well as the other women of her clan, was often sent in after a battle to go through the pockets of the dead. Phoebe never liked doing this, and it was even worse now because she'd witnessed the men being slayed. It really bothered her and it made her wonder about warriors like Hawke. Did he feel upset by it, too?

"Ye seem so calm, Lady Clarista," said Phoebe in admiration. "If it were my husband who had been killed or captured, I would be frantic right now."

"I've lived through a lot of hard times, Phoebe, and you will, too. Have you ever been married?"

"Nay, my lady," she told the Englishwoman. "I have never even been kissed by a man before today." When she realized just what she said, her eyes darted upward and her mouth dropped open. "I mean . . . what I mean is –"

Lady Clarista smiled. "So my grandson kissed you, did he?"

"I didna say that," Phoebe blurted out, wishing now she wouldn't have revealed so much.

"Hawke tends to always want what he cannot have." Clarista walked over and started to braid Phoebe's hair.

"Oh, he doesna want me," she protested.

"I wouldn't be so sure about that," said Clarista in a knowing manner. "I noticed the way he spoke up for you in the courtyard and how he made sure my son didn't put you in the dungeon."

"I'm sure it was only because he was grateful since I tended to his wound."

"Aye," she said, tying a red ribbon on the end of Phoebe's long, black braid that hung halfway down her back. "I'm sure you two could be happy together if you tried."

"Me? Us?" Phoebe's hand slapped against her chest and she felt her heart beating rapidly beneath her palm. "Oh, nay, my lady. Hawke and I are enemies. We will never be together, I assure ye."

"Don't enemies marry for the purpose of an alliance?"

Phoebe turned to face Clarista. "I – I suppose so."

"How old are you, Phoebe?" asked the woman folding her hands in front of her.

"I am eight and ten years of age," she told the woman.

Clarista nodded. "You are ten years younger than Hawke. You are also past marrying age but still young enough to bear many children."

"Is that . . . guid or bad?" she asked, not knowing what the woman meant.

"No matter what happens, I just ask that you be patient and understanding with my grandson. He has some demons from the past that haunt him still. I'm afraid he might never overcome them."

"I dinna understand, my lady. What do ye mean?"

"Hawke has been married before and it ended horribly," she told Phoebe.

"Aye," she said, knowing what Clarista meant. Phoebe picked up the end of her braid and twirled it nervously between her fingers. "He was the MacKeefe who married my cousin, Osla, ten years ago."

"Aye. And because of his choices at the time, he has never been able to forgive himself for her death."

"The MacNabs say he killed her. Is this true?"

"Why don't you ask him?" said Clarista, putting the brush on the dressing table.

"How did it happen? Why would he kill her?"

Clarista picked up her skirts and headed to the door. "There are many stories, but only Hawke knows for sure what happened. It is not my place to say anything more. That is something you will have to ask him about yourself. But for now, I think we should go down and get something to eat in the great hall."

"Will Orrick be there?" asked Phoebe anxiously, wanting to learn about herbs and magical potions from the old sorcerer before she went home.

"Are you really a healer?" asked Clarista, holding the door.

"I am. But I am still learnin'. One of the reasons we were in MacKeefe territory was because I was lookin' for the mugwort plant that grows in the Lowlands. I see now I never should have asked my clansmen to veer off our path on the way back home."

"Your father knows the dangers that lie at the border. Why would he let you come here with just a few men to protect you?" asked Clarista.

Phoebe had said too much. She didn't want the MacKeefes to know that her father was bedridden or they'd realize the MacNab's defenses were weak. She'd taken the men and headed to the border to find the herbs she needed to heal him, without her father giving his permission. He hadn't even known that she left. Now she regretted coming to the border at all.

"I think I am hungry after all," she said, instead of answering the woman's question. "Shall we go to the great hall as ye've suggested?

* * *

PHOEBE FELT EXTREMELY uncomfortable sitting at the dais dressed in Lady Clarista's plaid. Even though the woman was English, she was the old laird's wife and dressed like a Scot as well. But Phoebe dressing like a MacKeefe just seemed wrong.

Everyone from the nobles to the servants glared at her, never letting her forget she was their enemy. With her stomach so upset, she found it hard to eat a thing.

"Where is Hawke?" she asked Clarista, looking around the room, but not seeing him anywhere.

Storm heard her and glanced down the table. "My son is restin'. After the meal, the sorcerer will see to his wound."

"A sorcerer that acts like a servant?" asked Phoebe, taking a nibble of the white bread.

"Orrick is a friend, no' a servant," said Storm in a low voice.

Clarista giggled. "It is so good to hear you say that, Storm. After all, I know how many years you rejected anything or anyone's actions that you couldn't explain."

"Will I get to talk to Orrick about herbs tonight?" asked Phoebe.

"Nay. In the mornin', perhaps," growled Storm. "Tell me, Phoebe, how much do ye think yer clan will demand for ransom? And are they bringin' my faither straight to Crookston Castle or goin' somewhere else first?"

"I – I'm no' sure," she said, looking down at her trencher, picking up a piece of cheese and popping it into her mouth. She had to be careful with her words. Any information she told the enemy could be used against her clan. She didn't want her father or her people to be in danger. "Are ye plannin' on attackin' Clan

MacNab?" she nonchalantly asked, picking up her goblet and bringing it to her mouth.

"Dinna tell her anythin'," said Aidan from the end of the table. "Remember, she's the enemy and can turn against us."

"Ye should ken, Aidan, since it happened to ye with a bonnie lassie," laughed his friend, Ian, taking a drink of wine.

Feeling very uncomfortable, Phoebe wanted to leave. "Lady Clarista, may I take Hawke some food and check on his wound?" she asked.

"I'm sure that would be fine." Lady Clarista looked over to Storm for his approval.

"Orrick will go with her and there will be a guard posted at the door at all times," said Storm. "And if anyone sees the lass tryin' to escape, stop her. She is all we have to barter for my faither. We canna let her escape or the chieftain is as guid as dead."

"I'm no' goin' to try to escape," Phoebe told Storm, although the thought was at the back of her mind.

"Orrick," called Storm with a wave of his hand. "Please escort Phoebe to my son's chamber and be sure to take a guard with ye."

"Aye, my laird," said the tall man with white hair and a long beard. He was dressed in a purple cloak that reached all the way to the ground. "This way, Lady Phoebe." Orrick held out his hand. He seemed spry and moved quickly for such an old man. "We'll stop in the kitchen on the way up there and pick up some raw meat."

"Hawke eats raw meat?" gasped Phoebe, thinking he was some sort of animal.

"Nay, but his hawk, Apollo, does," answered Orrick with a cackle. "I have a feeling the bird is concerned about Hawke and hasn't hunted without its master by its side."

Phoebe hurried from the dais and followed the old sorcerer, looking back over her shoulder to see the hatred in every one of the MacKeefes' eyes. Mayhap she should be locked in the dungeon for her own safety, because she wasn't at all sure that one of the MacKeefes wouldn't try to slit her throat as she slept just because she was a MacNab.

After feeding Hawke's bird, Phoebe accompanied the sorcerer to a tower room. They were being followed closely by one of the MacKeefe's guards.

"What's up here?" asked Phoebe curiously as Orrick reached for the latch on the thick wooden door.

"This is where I stay when I'm at Hermitage Castle."

"Is this yer permanent residence?"

"Nay. I am usually at Blake Castle in Devonshire, but I visit here often."

"Devonshire? Ye're English, are ye no'?"

"I am."

"Then why are ye in Scotland?"

"You ask a lot of questions for a prisoner. I am good friends with Corbett Blake, an English lord. He is the brother of Storm MacKeefe's wife, Wren."

"Wren?"

"Hawke's mother."

"I dinna remember meetin' her."

"Nay, she is not here now. She is at the MacKeefe camp in the Highlands. The MacKeefes have two places where they stay interchangeably."

"I see," she said, wondering about Hawke's mother and wanting to learn more. But when the sorcerer opened the door and she got a glimpse inside, she forgot all about it. "This is amazin'." She anxiously followed Orrick into his tower room, noticing the guard stayed outside the door.

Shelves lined every wall inside the tower. Books, candles, crystals and gemstones filled the shelves. There even looked to be jars of herbs and things she couldn't identify. It was a mysterious place and she longed to see more.

"Aye, this is where I work." Orrick lit a candle even though light was coming in through the open window. Infatuated by the room, Phoebe hurried inside.

"I'll be right outside the door," said the guard, doing something that puzzled her. He reached over without stepping directly into the room and closed the door, leaving her alone with the sorcerer.

"He's no' comin' in the chamber?" she asked, not sure how she felt about being alone in a room with a strange man.

"Nay. It seems there are a lot of Scots as well as English who are superstitious. They fear me and want nothing to do with anything that might be considered magic."

"Can ye do magic?" she asked excitedly, being fascinated and not frightened at all.

Orrick looked at her from the sides of his eyes and headed across the room to some jars on the shelves. "There is nothing magical about healing herbs. They are nature's gift for us to use, but most people don't believe it."

"Oh, I do," she told him excitedly. "I've been studyin' herbs, but our healer back home canna teach me the things I want to learn."

"What is it you'd like to know? Perhaps I can help you."

"Would ye?" Phoebe's heart fluttered with excitement. Never would she have the chance to learn from a sorcerer again. Perhaps he could tell her what she needed to heal her father. However, she couldn't come out and ask him. If she told him the sad state of her father's condition, he might relay the information to the MacKeefes. Then they'd attack the MacNabs knowing their defenses were low. Nay, she had to do it in a roundabout way without asking him directly. "I would love to learn everythin' ye ken."

"Everything?" The sorcerer chuckled, pulling several jars from the shelves. "It would take years for that."

"How many years did it take ye?" she asked. "Ten? Twenty? Fifty?"

His hand stilled over one of the jars and the smile faded from his face. "It would take hundreds of years to gain the knowledge I have."

"Hundreds?" Phoebe laughed. "That canna be. After all, ye have the knowledge and ye are only . . . how old are ye?"

"Age is only a state of mind," said the sorcerer. "It doesn't matter. Now, let's get the herbs we need to heal Hawke and be on our way. What do you use to heal wounds?"

"I've been usin' comfrey made into a salve," she told him. "And of course, sage, thyme and St. John's wort, too."

"Those are all good, but there are other herbs that will work faster." He opened a jar and showed her a cream mixture.

"What is it?" she asked, peering at the ointment, taking a sniff.

"This is self-heal," he explained. "It's mixed with goldenrod and butter to help heal wounds."

"Is there anythin' else it's used for?" Wondering if it would be good to help her father's internal problems, she had to know more.

"The leaves are used for sore throats or ulcers in the mouth. And a bruised leaf of self-heal can stop the flow of blood if one is cut."

"What about this?" she asked, pointing to a jar with a dried herb in it that looked to have had pinkish white flowers at one time.

"That's valerian," he told her. "It helps nerves, stress and headaches and can cause one to sleep."

"Oh, that sounds handy."

"Beware," he warned her, taking a dried sprig from the jar and putting it into his pouch and then screwing the lid back on. "Too much of this can be very dangerous. You shouldn't use it if you don't know what you're doing."

"How about mugwort? Do ye have some of that?" she asked excitedly. "I came to the border lookin' for it, but couldna find any."

"I do," he said with a nod of his head, pulling down a wooden box and opening the lid. "What do you need it for?"

"I've heard it can keep disease away," she told him, wanting more than anything to bring some back to hopefully use to cure her father.

"Not only disease, but it'll keep away insects as well." He picked up a sprig between two fingers, studying it, and twirling it around. "Did you know this was used by the Druids?"

"Really?" This made her feel a little apprehensive since Druids were supposedly pagan. "What did they do with it?"

"It helps to promote psychic abilities." He handed her the sprig and she took it. "Put it under your pillow for it to work. It'll bring about sweet dreams."

"Oh. Thank ye," she said, opening her pouch and carefully placing it inside. "What about internal problems. Do ye have anythin' that will cure that?"

"Phoebe, do you want to tell me your real reason for asking these questions?"

"What do ye mean? I'm just curious and want to learn," she said, not able to look at him or he'd know she was lying. She only hoped he didn't have psychic abilities or he might be able to read her mind.

"To answer your question, yes there is an herb that will heal internal problems."

"Do ye have some?" she asked anxiously. "Can I see it?"

He pulled down a nearly empty jar. On the parchment that was tied around it, were written the words Hart's Tongue. There was one small dried plant inside.

"There is only one left," she said, bewildered as to why it wasn't replenished.

"That's right," he said. "Hart's Tongue can be used for internal problems. The leaves can also be made into an ointment for burns and scalds. It is very rare and hard to find, even though it grew abundantly in the hills hundreds of years ago."

"I see," she said, feeling heart-fallen. "Then I willna be able to find any on my own."

"Take this," he said, opening the jar and handing the dried herb to her.

"But . . . it's all ye have left."

"I have a feeling you know someone who needs it. But I will tell you that it will not work correctly unless combined with Common Centaury."

"Common?" she asked. "Oh, guid, then that should be easy to find."

"Not so," he said with a shake of his head. "The only place these herbs are found today are on the Isle of Kerrera."

"Isle of Kerrera? Where is that? Is it far?" she asked, feeling as if her good luck had just run out.

"It is a short boat ride from the MacKeefe camp that is in the Highlands near Oban."

"Really," she said, feeling her heart sink since she had no idea how she'd get there without a boat.

"The plants need to be harvested just as they're blooming."

"When is that?" she asked.

"It is happening now, for about a fortnight yet." Orrick pulled out a chair and sat down, nodding for her to do the same. "They need to be made into a tincture as a bitter tonic, and then ingested to cleanse the organs. I've used this concoction on people that have been near death and it cured them. I put it in whisky a few times, so the bitter taste was disguised."

"I see." She sat down across from him, looking down at the empty jar, feeling as if she were going to cry. Being a prisoner here, she wasn't even sure she'd be able to escape and get back home before the plant was finished blooming.

"It isn't impossible," he told her as if he could read her mind.

"Thank ye. I suppose we'd better see to Hawke now."

He reached over on the table and picked up a small leather-bound book and handed it to her.

"What is this?" she asked.

"It is my book of potions and tinctures to help heal those in need."

She flipped open the cover and was surprised to see a drawn picture of an herb. The name and everything it is used for as well as how to prepare it was listed next to it. "This is very informative," she said in awe, flipping through the book. Page after page was filled with pictures of herbs and writings that told about the plants and even where to find them. She felt honored that the sorcerer would share this with her.

"Take it with you," he told her. "But I want it back someday."

"Oh, I couldna," she said, closing the book and running her fingertips reverently over the leather covering. There was an engraving of a plant on the cover, and behind it was a bright star.

"Learn what you need in order to heal your loved one."

Her head snapped up in surprise. "How did ye ken?"

"Anyone who is as determined as you, must have someone they care about that they want to cure."

"I do," she admitted, but said nothing more.

"Please take care of it, and don't let it fall into the wrong hands. Some of the herbs are poisonous, and that is knowledge that could be dangerous if an enemy got hold of it."

"But . . . I am a MacNab. I am yer enemy," she reminded him. "Yet, ye give this to me anyway? Why?"

"I don't believe you are the enemy. Besides, you remind me of someone I once knew who was very special to me. Phoebe, I can see the future sometimes, and I see you being part of the MacKeefe Clan someday."

"Nay!" she spat, not wanting that to be true. After all, the MacKeefes were responsible for her cousin, Osla's death. "I promise ye, that'll never happen."

"Don't make promises you won't be able to keep."

She didn't know what that meant and neither did she care. She opened up the pouch that was slung over her shoulder, being held by a long strap. Then, carefully, she placed the book right next to the mugwort. "I dinna ken how I can ever repay ye, Orrick."

"You can repay me by bringing me some Common Centaury from the Isle of Kerrera when you return my book."

"But . . . I'm no' goin' to the Isle of Kerrera," she told him. "I am a prisoner here, and that is impossible."

"Nothing is impossible if you believe it can be so." The man spoke with wisdom, sounding as if he knew something about the future that she didn't. "Shall we go and tend to Hawke's wound now?" He got up and led the way across the room.

Orrick blew out the candle before reaching over to open the door. A shiver ran up Phoebe's spine and she felt as if something was going to happen, but she didn't know what. As she left the room, she wondered if she would ever be able to repay the sorcerer's kindness. But the Isle of Kerrera was so far away from here. Even if she did manage to escape, she'd never be able to get to the isle and back with the rare herb before her father passed away.

CHAPTER 8

Hawke brushed away something wet tickling his nose, opening one sleepy eye and then the other. He almost jumped out of his skin when he found four beady eyes staring at him and two long tongues lapping out to lick him once again.

"Egads, stop that!" He jerked upward to a sitting position, forgetting momentarily that he'd taken a blade to the shoulder yesterday. The pulling of his stitches and the sharp pain reminded him. "God's toes!" he ground out through gritted teeth. His hand shot to his wound and his eyes darted back to the wolf and the wolfhound standing on the bed staring at him. They were panting in his face.

"Och, ye're awake." Logan sat leaning back on a chair with his legs stretched out and resting on the bed. Ethan leaned against the bedpost cradling a tankard in his hand.

"I told ye he wasna dead," said Ethan. "And Jack and Trapper just proved it."

"Of course I'm no' dead, but ye two will be if ye try a stunt like that again," Hawke warned them. "Off the bed," he commanded, and both the animals leapt to the floor and disappeared in the shadows. He stared at Logan.

"What?" asked Logan, having no idea what he meant.

"I was talkin' to ye, no' the mutts. Get yer feet off my bed."

"Calm down and have somethin' to drink," said Ethan, handing him his tankard while Logan reluctantly moved his feet to the floor.

"How long have I been sleepin'?" asked Hawke, running a hand through his long, tangled hair. He took the tankard from Ethan, thinking it was ale or whisky and chugged some down.

"It's already mornin'," said Ethan, picking up a hunk of bread from the table, taking a bite and then giving the rest of it to his dog. Logan's wolf howled in protest.

As soon as Hawke swallowed, he realized he was drinking red wine. He spit out what was left in his mouth and threw the tankard to the floor. The wolf ran over to investigate and lick it up.

"Come here, Jack," said Logan, holding out his hand. "That madman might hurt ye."

"Aye, why are ye throwin' tankards around the room?" asked Ethan.

"Ye ken damn well I dinna drink red wine." He hadn't drunk red wine since he'd seen the blood covering Osla as she lay dead at his feet. Now, red wine only reminded him of that awful day.

Hawke wiped his mouth with the back of his hand, eyeing up Logan's tankard that he'd just raised to his mouth. "What are ye drinkin', Logan?"

Logan's eyes opened wide and he hurriedly downed the contents in three swigs. When he was finished, he made a smacking noise with his mouth and held the vessel upside down to show him it was empty. "It was Mountain Magic, but sorry, it's all gone now."

"What are ye two even doin' in my chamber and where is Orrick?" Aggravated and feeling like the devil, Hawke padded over to the window in his bare feet and pulled open the shutter. Bright sunlight shone in, hurting his eyes. He squinted and turned his head, closing the shutter again.

"We're here to make sure ye dinna die," said Ethan.

"That's right." Logan started to put his feet back up on the bed, but noticed Hawke's scowl and returned them to the floor. "Orrick and the girl were here with ye most of the night. Then we took over so they could get some sleep."

"The girl?" he asked. "Was Phoebe here, too? Where is she? Ye were supposed to help me keep an eye on her since she's our prisoner."

"Dinna fash yerself," said Ethan, shoving a sweetmeat into his mouth and throwing something that looked like real meat to both the dog and the wolf. "Caleb's watchin' her, so we're guid."

At that, the door burst open and Caleb hurried into the room, cradling something in his hands. "G'mornin'," he said with a wide smile on his face.

"That depends," said Hawke. "If ye've watched over the prisoner as instructed, then it's a guid mornin'. If no', someone has a lot of explainin' to do."

"Prisoner?" Caleb frowned. "Oh, if ye mean Phoebe, dinna worry about her. She's in her chamber sleepin' and there's a guard at the door." He opened his hands a little and peeked at something and then closed them again.

"Ye're sure of it?"

"Aye," answered Caleb. "I'm sure she's tired after sittin' up all night with the sorcerer talkin' about herbs. They used some potion to heal ye."

"Potion?" Ethan looked up and his eyes darted back and forth. "They didna do anythin' . . . like . . . magic, did they? It's said those spells can conjure the devil. A demon spirit can enter yer body and take control of yer soul."

"Magic isna real and ye need to stop bein' so superstitious," grumbled Hawke as he got dressed. Ethan continued eating.

Logan walked over and grabbed some food off the platter as well.

"I agree," said Logan. "Ye need to stop bein' such a scared wench, Ethan."

"I'm no' a scared wench. I just dinna want to tempt fate."

"Well, ye dinna have to fash yerself about the devil enterin' yer body," said Hawke, pulling on a boot. "After all, there's no room left in there for anythin' since ye filled yer body with my food to break the fast." Hawke walked over and looked down at the empty platter. Logan licked his fingers and Ethan threw the last of a crust of bread to his wolfhound. "Well, I hope one of ye at least thought to make sure Apollo was fed."

Logan and Ethan looked at each other and shrugged.

"I saw Orrick and the girl feedin' yer hawk," said Caleb, opening his hands a little and peeking inside.

"What in the name of the clootie have ye got there?" asked Hawke, thinking Caleb was acting like a fool.

"Well," said Caleb, sounding excited. "Ye ken how ye three are always tellin' me I need a pet?"

"Aye," said Logan. "What about it?"

"It so happens that this mornin' I found one."

"Ye have yer pet in yer hands?" asked Ethan. "It's that small?"

"It's perfect, I tell ye." Caleb sounded excited. "I wanted somethin' unique and I think I found it."

"Quit actin' so giddy and show us what ye've got," grumbled Hawke.

"All right," said Caleb, opening his hands to show them the rodent.

"A mouse?" Ethan and Logan started laughing uncontrollably.

"It's no' a mouse. It's a vole," said Caleb as if it mattered.

"It's a mouse," said Hawke, thinking that only Caleb would pick a rodent for a pet.

"It's a vole, I tell ye," said Caleb. "Ye can tell because its tail is shorter and hairier and its head is rounder."

"Where the hell did ye get that?" asked Logan, laughing. "From the gong pit?"

"Nay." Caleb frowned at his friends. "I found the little critter in my shoe this mornin'."

Jack ran over and jumped up on Caleb. The vole squeaked and darted out of Caleb's hands, hitting the floor. Then Trapper ran over and started barking. The vole took off across the floor, running out the open door with Trapper and Jack chasing it. Logan and Ethan laughed so hard that they were bent over and holding their stomachs.

"Caleb, pick another pet," said Hawke. "Ye ken my hawk is only goin' to eat it."

"Och, I forgot about that," said Caleb looking severely disappointed.

"How are you feeling today, Hawke?" came a female voice from the door.

Hawke looked up to see his grandmother standing there. "Better," he admitted, yawning, feeling like he needed more sleep. "Have ye seen Phoebe?"

"Nay, not this morning," answered Clarista. "I suppose she is still sleeping. I noticed the guard at her door when I walked by."

"Let her sleep," said Hawke. "But I'm starved and need food."

"Now I know you're feeling better," said Clarista with a smile. "Come on down to the kitchen. The meal is already over but I had the cook put aside a big portion of skirlie as well as black pudding since I knew you'd be hungry."

"Sounds guid to me," said Hawke, thinking of adding an extra goose egg to the oatmeal. He stopped and turned back, looking at Caleb. "Did ye want to join me, Caleb? After all, ye might get lucky and find a goose that hasna been killed yet to use as yer next pet."

The men all laughed, except Caleb who pushed past him and hurried out the door.

* * *

PHOEBE HADN'T MEANT to sleep so late, but she'd been up reading by candlelight most of the night. The book that Orrick had loaned her was fascinating. She'd learned more about healing herbs than she ever thought she would.

After dressing, she reverently picked up the leather-bound book in two hands and gently placed it in her bag. Then she went back to the bed and slipped her hand beneath the pillow to collect the dried sprig of mugwort. She held it up and smiled. Orrick had told her that it would give her good dreams and possibly let her see the future. Well, her dreams had been about kissing Hawke all night long. Unfortunately, she knew that since they were enemies, it was not going to be her future.

She carefully slipped the herb into the bag, thinking of everything they did to heal Hawke last night. Orrick had given Hawke a tincture that had valerian mixed in, so that he would sleep and his wound could heal.

After putting the strap of her bag over her shoulder, she headed to the door thinking about Hart's Tongue, Common Centaury, and the Isle of Kerrera. She had to find a way to get to the isle because the herb wouldn't be blooming long and without it, her father might die.

She pulled open the door to find the guard standing there. Sighing, she realized she was never going to be able to escape if she were being guarded every moment of the day. "I need to use the garderobe," she told him, thinking up a plan.

"I'll escort ye," said the guard, following her down the corridor to the opposite end of the castle where the garderobes were.

"There's no need to wait for me," she said, once they approached the door that led to the privy. "I'll join ye down in the great hall when I'm done."

"Nay. I have my orders and am no' to leave ye alone for a minute."

"Well now," she said, clearing her throat. "I suppose that means ye'll have to come into the privy with me and watch?"

The man made a face. "Nay. I'll wait here. Just hurry."

She turned and opened the door to the garderobe, covering her nose as she entered. One door led to six holes in a wooden bench with openings underneath. The urine and feces dropped down a chute and into an area behind the castle known as the gong pit that collected all the human waste. Once a week, a gong farmer came with his cart and shovels and rakes to empty it out.

In the hallway leading to the seats were poles with gowns and clothes hanging on them. By keeping the clothes so close to the smelly garderobe, it kept the moths away so the garments wouldn't get ruined. She stopped just inside and looked back to see two men approach the guard and start talking. One of them held a bottle of whisky and handed it to him. When he raised it to his lips to take a swig, Phoebe snuck out and hid in the shadows. And when one of the men started talking about a naked blond and the men all leaned in to hear better, Phoebe used it to her advantage and snuck down the back stairs.

Hurriedly, she made her way outside, almost gagging from the smell of the gong pit as she passed by, making her way toward the front gate. She was sure to stay hidden in the shadows. If she took her horse, she would be spotted riding out over the drawbridge. So instead, she decided, she would have to find someone else to ride her horse out of the gate and she would sneak out on foot.

"Ye there," she called out to a young boy playing in the dirt. He looked to be about six years old.

"Me?" the boy looked up in surprise.

"Come here," she said, pulling a shilling out of her pouch. "How would ye like this?"

The boy's eyes lit up. "I do." He grabbed for it, but she pulled back her hand with the coin in it.

"Ye've got to do somethin' for me first."

"What?" asked the boy.

"Go to the stable and find the tan horse with the black spot on its side. Then ride it out of the castle and meet me outside the gate. Then I'll give ye the coin."

"All right," said the boy, taking off at the run for the stable.

"This will be easier than I thought," said Phoebe, checking for her throwing knife hidden in her boot and also the one attached to her leg that she'd managed to keep hidden from Lady Clarista when she'd changed her clothes. Then she headed off in the shadows, making her escape.

* * *

HAWKE DECIDED to check on Apollo before he ate. Heading across the courtyard toward the mews, he was almost trampled as a young boy ran into him.

"Whoa, there, Harry," said Hawke, knowing all the children from the village as well as the ones who lived inside the castle walls. He loved children and they loved him as well. "Where are ye off to in such a hurry this mornin'?"

"I need to get to the stable right away," said the boy. His clothes were filthy and he had a streak of mud across the freckles on his little face.

"The stable?" Harry was the son of one of the serfs who used the castle kitchen to bake her bread. He lived in the village and wasn't a stableboy. "What have ye got to do of such importance that ye are in a hurry to get there?"

"A lady is goin' to give me a coin if I bring her horse to her outside the gate."

"Oh really," he said with a chuckle. "That must be a very generous lady to do that."

"I canna mount the horse without help. Will ye lift me, Hawke?"

Hawke realized the boy meant it and wasn't just playing a game.

"What did this generous lady look like?" he asked curiously.

"She was a bonny lady with a nice smile."

"What color was her hair and what was she wearing?"

"Her hair was dark and long and she wore the MacKeefe plaid."

"Did ye ever see her here at the castle or in the village before?" asked Hawke, having a feeling he knew who it was.

"Nay, my laird."

"Where did she want ye to bring the horse?"

"Just outside the castle gate. Will ye help me? She is waitin' and I dinna want to disappoint her."

"Nay, we wouldna want to disappoint her, now, would we?" Hawke looked around the courtyard and rubbed his chin. "Did she describe the horse ye are to bring to her?"

"She said it is tan with a black spot on its side."

"Phoebe's horse," he muttered under his breath. "How much money did she offer ye to do this?"

"A whole shillin', my laird." The boy's eyes lit up. This was a lot of money for someone so poor. Children didn't usually have money at all.

"I'll tell ye what." Hawke dug into his sporran, pulling out a silver coin and holding it up. The boy's eyes grew wide. "I'll give ye a merk if ye let me take the horse to the lady instead."

"All right," said Harry, nodding and holding out his hand.

"Here ye go," said Hawke, giving it to him and patting the boy on the head. He chuckled to himself and headed to the stable. The wench was sneaky, but she'd have a big surprise when he showed up with her horse instead.

CHAPTER 9

Phoebe waited in the shadow of a large wych elm tree just outside the castle gate. It was taking the boy too long and she started to think he wasn't going to show. But then she heard the clip clop of hooves over the drawbridge and saw a flash of tan of her horse through the trees. She smiled, thinking how easy this had been. All she had to do now was to collect her horse and ride west. She'd be halfway to Glasgow before anyone even knew she was missing.

Stepping out from behind the tree, she clutched the shilling in her hand. "It's about time ye got here," she said, stopping dead in her tracks when she saw Hawke staring down at her from atop her horse instead of the boy.

"Goin' somewhere, my lass?" he asked, making her heart sink. She'd been caught and now he'd probably throw her in the dungeon for sure.

"Hawke," she said, flashing a smile. She accidentally dropped the shilling and it thudded against the hard ground.

"Next time ye plan an escape, ye'd better ask someone who's tall enough to mount a horse by himself. And by all means, offer them a little more than a shillin'."

"I wasna tryin' to escape. I was just . . . goin' out ridin' and lookin' for herbs."

"Please dinna insult me with that lie. We both ken ye were tryin' to run away. Now get on the horse and let's get back inside the castle walls." He held out his hand and waited.

Phoebe sighed, knowing it was senseless to try to run. He'd catch her before she even made it to the woods. With no other choice, she picked up her coin and reached up and took his proffered hand. Hawke easily hoisted her into the saddle in front of him.

"The old sorcerer and I tended to yer wound last night, but ye didna waken," she said, trying to take the attention off the fact she truly was trying to escape.

"Aye, and I thank ye," he said, slipping his arm around her waist as he turned and headed back to the castle.

"So, ye are feelin' better then?" she asked.

"I am."

"And yer wound is healin'?"

"It is."

The cry of his hawk from above told her that she was being watched by both Hawke and Apollo now. "Ye canna blame me," she said with a sigh. "After all, if ye were bein' held prisoner by my clan, ye would try to escape, too."

"The MacNabs would never be able to catch me," he told her, sounding so arrogant that it made her roll her eyes.

"Well, they were able to abduct yer laird," she pointed out.

"That's only because my grandda is no' the man he used to be. He's been slowin' down a lot in the past few years. If it were my da with me yesterday instead, yer men wouldna have taken a prisoner at all. Neither would a one of them have walked away alive."

"Ye think ye are untouchable, but if I must remind ye, ye almost died. And if ye would have died like ye were supposed to, then I wouldna be a prisoner right now at all."

"What kind of talk is that?" he spat. "It almost sounds as if ye wanted me to die."

"Ye deserve to die for killin' my men."

"Yer men attacked me first, or have ye forgotten? Plus, it was four against one. I was fightin' for my life."

"Well, then ye deserve to die for killin' Osla."

His body stiffened at her words and his arm tightened around her waist. "What do ye ken about that?" he asked, not sounding happy at all.

"Osla was no' only my cousin, but she was also my best friend," she told him. "I was only a child when ye married her, but I cried every day when ye took her away."

"Osla," he said, seeming to get choked up at hearing her name. "I didna kill her, lass," he said under his breath. "That's no' what happened at all."

"That's no' what the MacNabs say."

"Well, they're lyin'." Now he seemed to be getting very angry.

"If ye try to kill me like ye did her, I swear I'll kill ye first."

"Is that a threat?" he asked in a gruff voice, his hot breath in her ear. He was masculine and strong, and she felt affected sitting so close to him. Even though he was her enemy, she oddly felt attracted to him, which only made things worse.

"It's a warnin'," she whispered back, closing her eyes, trying to ignore his manly scent of pine and musk. His strong arm held her tightly, and she was pressed up against his hard body, making her feel hot being so close to him right now.

"Dinna think ye could ever kill me, lass, because ye are sadly mistaken."

"Dinna be so sure," she whispered, resting her hand over her throwing knife tied to her thigh that was hidden under her gown. Even if she felt an attraction to this MacKeefe and couldn't stop thinking about the kiss they'd shared, he was still her enemy and also her captor. She needed to remember that. He was one of the most dangerous men alive. She'd seen the way he'd taken down four MacNabs without even breaking a sweat. He was a killer. A murderer, she reminded herself, her eyes filling with tears to think of poor Osla and how she died at the hands of her own husband.

Hawke had protected Phoebe and kept her from going to the dungeon. And for that, she was grateful. But she was a captive of the MacKeefes, and they severely misjudged her just because she was a girl. None of them had even thought to check her for weapons. Thankfully, she still had her throwing knives, and if she had to use them to escape, she wouldn't hesitate to do so. Even if her knife was aimed right at Hawke.

* * *

"Storm MacKeefe bravely set out with only a young squire to search the rugged hills of the Highlands for the band of renegades," read Bridget, holding the open book of the Highland Chronicles in front of her. Everyone gathered around her in the great hall, listening intently to the latest entry in the king's book. Her father sat next to her, smiling.

"Young squire?" Hawke blew air from his mouth, talking to Phoebe as they entered the great hall. "It was a French knight he had with him who was almost the same age as him."

"Mayhap the chronicler misunderstood," said Phoebe innocently.

"Or mayhap my faither embellished the story a little," remarked Hawke.

"Ye sound jealous." Phoebe's face lit up in a smug smile.

"Hardly."

"I dinna believe ye."

"Then dinna believe me, because it doesna matter to me at all what ye think."

"Read the part about me again," said Hawke's grandfather, Callum. "I want to hear about my Mountain Magic."

"Aye, read that part, Bridget," Brigham told his daughter. "My daughter always reads my works aloud," the man explained to the crowd. "She has a nice voice and an excitin' way of bringin' the stories to life."

The girl flipped back a page and thumbed her finger over the parchment, stopping halfway down. *"Callum MacKeefe is the eldest and wisest, most experienced member of the clan,"* she read, getting a huge smile from Hawke's great-grandfather. *"His potent Mountain Magic is his original recipe for his strong Scottish whisky that he brews in secret in a cave."*

"He does?" asked Phoebe curiously.

"He used to, when he was considered addled and was hidin' away from everyone," Hawke told her.

"This Mountain Magic is revered and coveted by people all the way from the bonnie hills of the Highlands to the sandy coast of southern England. It has even been kent to render the Scots' enemies unconscious for days at a time. It is the MacKeefe's secret weapon for winnin' battles."

"Really?" asked Phoebe in awe.

"I suppose it has been used several times to slow down our enemies," agreed Hawke. "And my da drank too much and passed out for a few days, but that is nothin' to boast about. Och, I've heard enough. Let's go."

"It also has medicinal qualities, and has brought about miraculous recovery of bad health and is also attributed to longevity," read Bridget. *"Some say it is a secret potion that can possibly lead to immortality."*

"Wait!" Phoebe stopped dead in her tracks and put her hand on Hawke's arm to keep him from leaving. Hawke liked the feel of her touch. His eyes dropped to her long, slim fingers. Thoughts ran through his head and he found himself fantasizing that she was holding on to his arm as his lady and he was her man. Shaking the absurd thought from his head, he heard Bridget's next words.

"Auld Callum MacKeefe drinks Mountain Magic every day and this is what has kept him alive for nearly a hundred years. His magic potion might make him live another hundred."

"He's a hundred years auld?" gasped Phoebe. "That is unheard of to live that long."

"Nay, he's no'," grunted Hawke, making a face. "That is wrong. Way wrong."

"Then how auld is he?" she asked.

"I dinna ken," said Hawke with a shrug of his shoulders. "I'm no' sure anyone really does, but I'd guess he isna a day over ninety at most."

"Ninety? Years auld? Hawke, that is remarkable. No one lives that long. Mayhap his whisky has given him longevity after all."

"It's more likely his ornery nature is what has cheated death."

A woman screamed from the other end of the great hall, and Hawke's head snapped around in alert. "Somethin's wrong," he said, noticing chaos starting and women hiding behind their men. His hand was instantly on the hilt of his sword. "I'm goin' to find out what it is." He took two steps away and then turned back and grabbed her hand. "Ye're comin' with me where I can see ye at all times."

Hawke pushed his way between the crowds of people, hurrying across the hall. And as he emerged, he saw Caleb standing there with a smile on his face and a yellow and brown striped snake wrapped around his arm.

"Caleb, what are ye doin'?" asked Hawke.

"How do ye like my new pet?" Caleb held up his arm with the snake attached. A couple more of the ladies screamed and hid behind their men.

"Caleb's got a snake?" Logan pushed to the front of the crowd with Ethan at his side.

"Caleb, that could be poisonous," said Ethan. "It's no' safe."

"Nay, it's no' venomous," Caleb assured them, running a finger over it as if he were petting it.

"How do ye ken?" asked Logan.

"It's smooth, instead of having scales, and its colorin' is solid instead of havin' a jagged pattern. Plus, poisonous snakes have oblong, slit-lookin' pupils and this one has round ones. See?" He stepped toward Logan and Ethan, shoving the snake in their faces. They quickly stepped backward to get away from it.

"Caleb, ye fool, ye dinna choose somethin' like that for a pet," Hawke told him.

"Well, ye said a vole wasna a guid choice and that I should choose a predator and so I did."

"Get rid of it. Ye're scarin' all the lassies," Hawke told him.

"I thought this was perfect when I found it under the log in the garden this mornin'."

"Well, it's no'," said Hawke.

"Fine. I'll just find somethin' else then." With his head down and everyone parting and giving him room to walk, Caleb left the great hall with his snake, scowling like a reprimanded child.

"Hawke, I think it's time to take a look at your wound." Orrick walked up to meet them.

"I'm fine," said Hawke, his hand going to his shoulder.

"Is that true, Phoebe?" Orrick looked to the girl for his answer.

"Now, how would she ken the answer to that when she was too busy tryin' to escape?" asked Hawke.

"Who's tryin' to escape?" Unfortunately, Hawke's father overheard them and headed over. "Hawke, dinna ye understand that our only hope of gettin' Ian back is if we have MacNab's daughter for a trade?"

"I do, Da," said Hawke. "Have the MacNabs sent a messenger yet with either a ransom letter or an offer of a trade?"

"No' yet," said Storm. "But I am sendin' one of our messengers to Crookston Castle today. We canna wait for them to make the first move. Each day Ian is gone, he is one day closer to death and we are one day closer to a battle."

"I still say we should storm their castle and take grandda back by force," said Hawke.

"I agree," added Ethan.

"Nay, it's too dangerous," Storm told them.

"Let us go," Logan urged him. "Hawke, Ethan, Caleb and I can be in and out and back with our chieftain before they even ken what happened."

"And what about her?" Storm nodded toward Phoebe. "What do ye think they'll do when we rescue Ian and keep MacNab's daughter?"

"Aye, I suppose that would be a problem," said Ethan with a shrug.

"We need to keep her close," said Storm. "If they do no' go for a trade then our only choice is to make an alliance and have one of ye marry the girl."

PHOEBE'S HEAD snapped up at hearing that suggestion. She didn't like it one bit. There was no way she was going to marry a MacKeefe. They were the MacNabs' enemies. Besides, with her luck, they'd betroth her to Hawke and she'd end up dead just like her cousin.

"I willna marry any of ye," she retorted.

"Really?" Hawke asked with a chuckle. "And what will ye do when the MacNabs refuse to make a trade and tell us to keep ye, just like yer clan members did when I captured ye?"

"They didna mean it," she said, feeling very nervous. "My faither will make the trade. I'm sure he will. There will be no need for a battle or to make an alliance."

Phoebe looked from one MacKeefe to the next, not able to picture herself as the wife of any of them. She hoped her father's health was getting better and that he wasn't already dead. Because if Euan and Lennox were in charge, she had no chance at all of coming back to the clan unmarried.

CHAPTER 10

"Hold still so I can change the bandage and check yer stitches," Phoebe told Hawke that night after they had retired to his solar.

"Are ye sure ye ken what ye are doin'?" asked Hawke.

"I told ye, I am still learnin' but ye need no' worry. Orrick loaned me his book and I've been readin' it and learnin' a lot."

"What book?" he asked as Phoebe finished her ministrations. "I hope it's no' a book of spells. I dinna want ye cursin' me."

"Now why would I do that?" she asked, putting the ointments back into her bag.

"Because we're enemies and ye had no qualms in admittin' that ye'd like to see me dead?"

"Nonsense." She peeked under his bandage and applied more cream. "If I wanted to kill ye, ye'd be dead by now."

"Now that's a reassurin' thought."

"Here's the book," she said, wiping off her hands and taking the book out of her travel bag. She reverently held it in two hands in front of Hawke.

"Ye act like ye're holdin' the king's crown or somethin'," he said with a chuckle. "I assure ye, it's only an auld book and holds no value."

"On the contrary, this book is very valuable to me."

"Why is that?" he asked, taking the book from her and thumbing through a few pages. "Plannin' on bein' a witch? After all, Orrick is a sorcerer so ye'd better be careful around him. I'm no' sure I even like the man. Ye'd better stay away from him for now."

"I think Orrick is a wonderful man to help me find the herbs I've been searchin' for. And ye have no idea how important this is to me." She tried to snatch the book away from him but he put it down next to him and lay back on the bed.

"Why is that, lass?" he asked, sounding suspicious of her. "Ye act like it's a matter of life or death."

"It might be," she said, feeling flustered just thinking about her father. "There are some herbs I need. To heal a very sick man back at Crookston Castle. I found out from Orrick that the herbs are only found in one place."

"And where's that?" he asked with a yawn. "Inside a magic lantern?"

"Stop it, Hawke! This is nothin' to be jestin' about when a man's life hangs in the balance."

"Ye're really upset about this." Hawke's face took on a serious expression.

"I am. But unfortunately, I'm a prisoner here and the herbs I need have to be picked while they're bloomin' or I'll have to wait another year. By then it'll be too late."

"Well, mayhap if yer clan hurries up and makes a trade and we get our chieftain back, then ye can go look for yer herbs." Hawke closed his eyes and rested his hands on his chest, not at all concerned.

"I wish that were true. But even if it happens, I'll have no way to get to the isle."

"The isle? What isle?" His eyes popped open.

"Orrick told me the only place the herbs grow are on the Isle of Kerrera which is a boat ride away from Oban."

"The Isle of Kerrera?" Hawke raised a brow. "I dinna think ye'll find anyone to take ye there."

"Why no'?" she asked.

"Because, the isle is said to have a haunted castle. Everyone kens that. No one goes there unless they are lookin' to meet ghosts or the devil himself."

"A haunted castle?" she asked, being intrigued and also a little scared. "Well, I dinna care. I'd go there to find the herbs. It's that important to me."

"Well, guid luck findin' someone to take ye there. Now come here, lass."

"Why?" she asked. "Is your wound hurtin'?"

"Nay." He sat up in the bed as she approached him. "I just need to make sure ye dinna try to escape again while I sleep."

"What are ye goin' to do?"

He reached over to the bedside table and pulled a skein of rope out of the drawer. Then he tied one end to her ankle.

"Ye are tyin' me up? Like a prisoner?" she asked.

"The last time I checked, ye were still a prisoner. And aye, I am tyin' ye to me."

"To ye?" Her heart sped up. What did he mean?

"I'm goin' to tie one end to yer foot and the other to mine. And I'm goin' to wrap the rope around the bedpost a few times in between."

"Ye are crazy!"

"I'm playin' it safe." He finished tying the rope and lay back down on the bed. Since there wasn't a lot of rope between her ankle and his, she had no choice but to go with him. "Lay down, lassie. It's easier to sleep that way."

"Next to ye?" she gasped.

"Aye, next to me. That's the idea."

"Ye'd better no' touch me as I sleep."

"I wouldna dream of it. Now come." He held out his hand to help her lie next to him on her back. She stared up at the ceiling, not able to ignore the fact the bed was small and her body was pressed up next to his. She felt the heat emanating from his skin. His musky scent mixed with the smell of wood smoke and the tangy healing herbs filled her senses.

"I dinna like this," she told him.

"I dinna like havin' to tie ye up, but ye've already proven to me that ye canna be trusted. Ye are the MacKeefes' only hope to get my grandfaither released. And as soon as our messenger returns from yer castle, we'll hopefully make the trade and we'll never have to see each other again."

"Guid. I'd like that," she said, feeling an emptiness in her chest. Why did the idea of never seeing Hawke again bother her so much? She closed her eyes and pretended to sleep, knowing she had to get away from here as fast as she could. She couldn't stay around Hawke any longer because he was confusing her mind.

"Guid night, my wee lass," said Hawke. And then she felt his lips touch hers in a gentle kiss. For a moment, she wanted to pull him closer and deepen the kiss and wrap her arms and legs around him. *He's yer enemy,* she reminded herself, breaking the kiss and pushing him away. Her eyes popped open.

"Blethers, careful, lass," he cried out. "Remember my wound!"

"Ye promised ye wouldna touch me."

"My hands came nowhere near ye. I didna ken ye meant my lips as well."

"Well now ye do." She closed her eyes and turned on her side, away from him, feeling more than ever now that she needed to escape as soon as she could.

* * *

When Phoebe heard Hawke snoring, she reached for her throwing knife tied to her leg. Then she sat up and reached down, sawing at the rope. Hawke tied a mean knot. If she didn't have this knife, she'd never be able to get loose. She had just about cut through the rope when Hawke coughed and moved. He turned on his side and she held her breath, hoping he wouldn't open his eyes and realize what she was doing. Her heart beat rapidly as she waited. Then, when he started snoring again, she cut through the rope, setting herself free.

Tying the end of the rope to his other leg, she did all she could to make it harder for him to chase after her if he should awake.

Quickly and quietly, she made her way to the table at the other side of the room. Thankfully, she saw that the servants had washed her clothes and returned them. They were folded and put into a neat pile. It was night and she only had the light from the nighttime candle to see, but it was all she needed.

Hurriedly, she dressed in her own clan's clothes, taking a cloak she found hanging on a hook to cover up the bright red plaid. It was a large, long cloak and she was sure it was Hawke's. Then she slipped the strap of her traveling bag over her shoulder. She was halfway to the door when she remembered Orrick's book. She'd promised to return it, but she still needed it. She needed the pictures of the herbs, and to learn everything he'd written inside.

Turning around, she spied the book on the bed, sticking out from under Hawke.

"Och, nay," she whispered, heading back to the bed. He was facing her, lying on his side. Slowly, she reached out for the book, laying her hands upon it. It was partially beneath his body and she'd have to pull it to get it out from under him. It didn't work. He was too heavy. She had to think of another way.

Picking up her long braid, she used the end of it to tickle his nose.

Immediately, his hand shot up to his face and she had to jump back so he wouldn't hit her. Then he dropped his hand back to the bed and she did it again. This time, he wrinkled his nose, made a face, and thankfully turned onto his other side.

Phoebe let out a breath of relief and grabbed the book. After slipping it into her pouch, she picked up the long ends of the cloak and hurried to the door. Opening it a crack, she saw a guard sitting on a chair with his eyes closed. Thankfully, he'd been drinking. She could see he had a bottle in his hand and the cork was on the floor.

After checking both ways, she sneaked out into the corridor, softly closing the door behind her. She was about to leave when she had an idea. Hadn't the writing in the Highland Chronicles said something about the MacKeefe's Mountain Magic knocking a man out for days? Mayhap she could use this to her advantage.

Reaching over the guard, she slipped the bottle out of his hand and picked up the cork from the floor. She took a quick sniff of the contents and knew immediately it was Mountain Magic. Smiling, Phoebe tucked the bottle into her pouch and headed down the hall. It looked as if she were going to be able to escape after all. She'd be free as soon as she got outside the castle gates. So why, she wondered, did she feel as if she'd let Hawke down?

CHAPTER 11

Hawke awoke the next morning to the sound of shouting from the courtyard. Having the reflexes of a warrior, he sprang from bed, but fell flat on his face on the ground. His feet were still up on the bed and tied together, not to mention they were tied to the bedpost, too.

"Phoebe!" he yelled, getting the attention of the guard in the hallway. The door opened and the guard stood there with wide eyes.

"What's the matter, my laird?" he asked.

"Where is she?" he ground out, trying to reach the ropes. But being on the ground with his feet still on the bed, it was difficult to free himself.

"Who?" asked the guard.

"The prisoner, ye fool."

"I – I dinna ken," he said. "I never saw her leave." The man stifled a yawn and cocked his head. "Why are ye tied up, my laird?"

"Get me out of this before I have yer head for fallin' asleep and lettin' her slip away."

"Aye, my laird." The guard used his dagger and started cutting the ropes just as Logan, Caleb, and Ethan ran in. They seemed as if they had just woken up and had wrinkled clothes and tousled hair.

"Hawke, did ye hear what's happenin'?" asked Caleb, stopping and eyeing him curiously. "What are ye doin'?"

"I tied Phoebe to me before I went to sleep so she wouldna escape," Hawke told them. "I also put a guard at the door and still she got away."

"A wench did that to ye?" asked Ethan, and the three of them started laughing.

"Haud yer wheesht and help me find her," growled Hawke. "I need to bring her back before my da finds out she escaped again."

"It's too late," said Logan, crossing the room and throwing open the shutter. The sun was just starting to rise. Shouts were heard from below and also the sound of running feet.

"What's all the commotion?" asked Hawke, getting free of the ropes and running over to the window. Everyone was in chaos. The courtyard was filled with people rushing to and fro, and he could see smoke on the horizon.

"King Richard is leadin' his English soldiers up the coast," said Ethan. "The Scots have already started burnin' their possessions and crops so the bluidy Sassenachs canna use them to their advantage."

"God's eyes, nay! Let's go," said Hawke, strapping on his weapons. When he went for his cloak, he realized it was gone. And there on the floor in a pile were the MacKeefe clothes that Phoebe had worn.

"Hawke, ye're no' goin' with us," said Storm, entering the room.

Hawke turned to face his father. "Why no'? We'll need to fight the English. Ye ken I am one of yer best warriors."

"I need ye to take the girl to the Highlands where she'll be safe. We canna risk anythin' happenin' to her before the return of yer grandfaither. With the English movin' in, Hermitage Castle bein' on the border is no' the safest place to be."

Silence enveloped the room as Storm's eyes scanned the area. "Where is the girl, Son?"

Hawke ran a weary hand through his hair and let out an exasperated sigh. "She's no' here, Da. But I'll find her. I promise I will."

"God's teeth, dinna tell me ye let her escape again?" A frown darkened Storm's face.

"I guess she must have had a dagger hidden in her clothes," said Hawke with a shrug. "I suppose I should have checked for one before I fell asleep."

"Dammit, Son, what is the matter with ye? Dinna ye realize this is the worst time for this to happen? With the English now on Scottish soil, we need Ian back more than ever. And now I canna even try for his return because there is a war at hand."

"I'll find her Da, I swear I will."

"I'm sure she's headed back to the MacNabs," said Storm. "It's on the way to the MacKeefe camp. Yer friends will go with ye. Find her and bring her to our camp in the Highlands and keep her there for now. Protect yer mathair and the women and children there as well. Renard will watch over Hermitage Castle. The Madmen MacKeefe will join me and the others and we'll head to the border to help. I've heard talk of a possible ambush by the Scots. I need to find out exactly what is goin' on."

"Let me go with ye, Da. I want to fight." Hawke always led the way in any battle or war. Fighting was what he knew best. To be told he couldn't go only made him angrier.

Storm shook his head. "Nay. It's yer fault the girl is gone and if ye dinna get her back, the death of yer grandfaither will be on yer conscience for the rest of yer life."

"I'll find her. I told ye I would. She couldna have gotten far in the dark."

"We'll help him," said Logan.

"Take Callum with ye," commanded Storm.

"What?" asked Hawke, not wanting to do this. "Great-grandda will only slow us down."

"I want him out of here if by any chance the English try to take Hermitage Castle. He is auld and canna fight. He'll only be a distraction and I canna afford to assign men to protect him. And Hawke, dinna let anythin' happen to yer mathair or yer sisters in the Highlands."

"I willna," said Hawke. "Ye can count on me."

"Aye, I am countin' on ye, Son. So dinna let me down again."

* * *

HAWKE WALKED into the stable to saddle a horse, stopping in his tracks when he saw Orrick sitting in the wagon next to Callum. "What is this?" he asked.

"We're ready to go back to the Horn and Hoof," Callum told him, talking about the tavern he owned in Glasgow where he sold his Mountain Magic.

"Orrick, why are ye in the cart?"

"I'm coming with you," said the sorcerer, making Hawke cringe. Having one old man along would slow them down. But with two of them, it was going to make it impossible to track and find Phoebe.

"Nay, ye stay here. There are already too many people in this travelin' party."

"But someone will have to tend to yer wound now that Phoebe is gone," said Orrick, making sense. If Hawke got an infection, things could turn for the worse. Besides, mayhap the sorcerer could use some of his magic in helping him find Phoebe.

"Fine, then. But both of ye will have to ride horses. The wagon will slow us down too much, no' to mention get us noticed faster by the MacNabs or the English."

"There are no extra horses," said Logan, walking into the stable with Caleb and Ethan at his side.

"What? Why no'?" asked Hawke.

"Yer faither says they need every horse possible for the soldiers headin' to the coast," explained Ethan.

Hawke looked around for Phoebe's horse, happy when he found it. When she escaped the castle, she must have gone on foot in order not to be discovered. "One of ye will ride Phoebe's horse," he told them.

"Nay," answered Ethan.

"What do ye mean, nay?" spat Hawke.

"Unless ye're forgettin', ye no longer have a horse since it was stolen by the MacNabs," Ethan continued. "So, ye'll have to ride it."

"Damn, that's right." Hawke shook his head in frustration. "All right, take the wagon," he told the men. "Do ye have supplies for all of us in there? It'll be a few days before we get to the camp."

"We have enough to get us to Glasgow," said Callum. "We couldna take more because there is no tellin' what will happen back here at Hermitage Castle. If the English try to lay siege to our stronghold, Renard and the others will be trapped inside and will need food."

"We'll make do without it then," said Hawke, readying Phoebe's horse. "We can hunt along the way. Leave everythin' here but the wine and ale, and one day's supply of food."

"Aye, my laird," said Orrick as he and Callum climbed out of the wagon to do as commanded.

"Which way do ye think Phoebe headed?" asked Ethan, climbing atop his horse. His wolfhound waited, lying by the door to the stable.

"She canna have gotten far without a horse," said Hawke, pulling himself up into the saddle. "She'll probably keep to the main road, so we'll take it toward Glasgow. We should have her back by sundown."

"I hope ye're right," said Callum as he and Orrick climbed up to the driver's seat of the wagon and Orrick took the reins. "Because if we dinna find her, ye are goin' to have to come up with another way to rescue our laird."

"I will, Great-grandda," said Hawke. "Ye just leave it to me."

Hawke headed out of the stable with the rest of the party following. Smoke filled the air from the coast and shouting was heard on the wind. They'd be heading in the opposite direction so this shouldn't be a problem. They'd only encounter trouble if bandits or the MacNabs decided to approach them.

Hawke hesitated and watched the party of men heading to the coast being led by his father. He should be with them to fight the English. Hawke wanted to protect his father as well as his clan. But because of the girl, he had no choice. With a sigh, he turned his steed and headed toward the Highlands instead.

* * *

PHOEBE'S FEET hurt like the devil and she now regretted not taking her horse. But if she had, she would have been spotted by the guards and would never have been able to sneak out of the castle without being seen.

Wiping her brow with her sleeve, she sat down on a rock to rest and remove a stone from her shoe.

"Damn ye, Hawke MacKeefe," she cursed aloud. "Why did ye ever have to capture me? Now I'll no' be able to make it to the isle to find the herbs to heal my faither."

The day had gone quickly during her journey and the sun was already starting to set. While it splashed beautiful colors of orange and red across the sky and hills, it concerned her greatly. She didn't know where she'd spend the night. It was dangerous being a woman on the road all alone, and especially at nighttime. These woods could be crawling with cutthroat bandits for all she knew. Why hadn't she found a way to bring the horse? What had she been thinking?

Hearing the sound of someone traveling down the road and getting closer, she quickly put her shoe back on, and hid behind a tree. Mayhap she could sneak onto the back of a peddler's wagon and hitch a ride so she'd at least have a place to sleep for the night. Peeking out from behind the tree, she saw two men approaching in a wagon. They wore hooded cloaks and were seated on a bench driving the cart. From her position, she could tell one had a long white beard and the other had wrinkled hands. But she couldn't see their faces because of their raised hoods. However, she was sure they were old. Even if they discovered her in their cart, she could sweet talk her way out of anything. They didn't look dangerous, so she decided to give it a try.

As soon as the wagon passed by the tree, she darted out after it. Hopping onto the back, she quickly lay down and rolled over so she would not be seen. When the cart didn't stop and she heard the men talking to each other, she realized her plan had worked. Staring up at the sky she smiled and let out a deep breath of relief. This was proving to be a lot easier than walking all the way back to Crookston Castle that was just outside of Glasgow. Phoebe noticed a red tail hawk up in the sky, making circles above her and her heart about stilled.

"Enjoyin' the ride?" Hawke emerged from behind some covered barrels inside the wagon, looking straight down at her.

"Hawke!" She bolted up to a sitting position and tried to scoot over to the end of the cart, but his hand clamped down on her wrist and kept her from leaving.

"I figured ye'd be tired about now and ready to find a ride. Ye are so predictable."

"Oh really?" she asked. "If that were true, ye would have kent I was goin' to escape. Yet, I had no problem sneakin' out while ye slept." She flashed him a sarcastic smile and he frowned.

"Hello, Phoebe," said Orrick from the driver's seat, lowering his hood and looking over his shoulder.

"Hello, Orrick," she replied.

"It's that MacNab wench that's nothin' but trouble," growled old Callum from the sorcerer's side, glancing back at her as well. He undoubtedly was not happy at all to see her.

Hawke peered down the road behind them as if he were looking for someone. Then he put his fingers in his mouth and whistled loudly.

Immediately, she heard the sound of hoofbeats pounding the earth. Then Caleb, Logan, and Ethan rode up, mounted on horses. The wolfhound and the wolf led the way. Caleb held the reins of her horse that she figured Hawke had probably been riding earlier.

"So, I see it takes six men, a wolf, and a hound to hunt me down," she said with a sniff. "It's no' impressive at all."

"Stop the wagon," Hawke called over his shoulder to Orrick. When it stopped, he stood up, bringing her with him. "It's no' impressive that ye keep lyin' to me and keep tryin' to escape."

"I managed to do it, and no' even yer guard stopped me, thanks to this." She proudly displayed the bottle she'd taken from the sleeping guard.

Hawke took it from her, uncorked it and took a swig. "Mountain Magic," he said with a smack of his lips, sounding satisfied.

"See? I told ye my Mountain Magic is strong as well as an important secret weapon," said Callum with a cackle from the front of the cart. "Guid thing I brought a barrel of it along for the trip."

"What trip? Where are ye goin'?" asked Phoebe. "I thought ye all came lookin' for me."

"Dinna flatter yerself, lass." Hawke stepped from the wagon to mount her horse. "Ye are just a diversion along the way. Now come." He held out his hand to her, but she shook her head.

"Nay. I'd rather no' ride with ye. I'll stay here in the back of the cart instead."

"Ye dinna have a choice. Now give me yer hand or I'll get off this horse and throw ye over my shoulder, so dinna think I willna do it."

"Oh, all right," she grumbled, giving him her hand and mounting the horse in front of him.

"Let's ride," Hawke called to the rest. "If we hurry, we can make it to Elvanfoot before sunset. We'll camp there for the night alongside the River Clyde. Then we'll stop off at Glasgow tomorrow before headin' home to MacKeefe territory."

"Glasgow?" asked Phoebe, interested to hear this, since it was near the MacNabs' castle. "We're stoppin' there?"

"Dinna get excited," Hawke said in a low voice, right next to her ear. "We're only droppin' off my grandda at the Horn and Hoof and we're no' goin' through MacNab territory to do it. Oh, and if ye think I'm takin' my eyes off of ye for one minute this entire trip, ye've got another guess comin'. Ye will stay with me every second and, this time, I willna be so foolish as to leave ye with a blade."

His hand snaked around her, grabbing her thigh and making her jerk.

"What are ye doin'?"

"I'm disarmin' ye, lass." His palm covered the knife right through her clothes that was strapped to her thigh. Then he used one hand and gripped her gown, pulling it upward, exposing her leg.

"Stop it!" She struggled in his arms.

"Sit still," he warned her, expertly using his fingers to slip the knife out of its sheath, holding it up in the air. "A throwin' knife?" he asked, sounding surprised, perusing her weapon.

"Aye. And I ken how to use it, too." Phoebe hurriedly pushed her gown back down to cover her leg.

"Is this the only one ye have or are there more?"

"Aye. Nay," she said, answering both of his questions at once.

"Well, which is it? Aye or nay?" he asked in a low voice.

"It's the only one."

"I dinna believe ye." He moved the reins to his hand that was holding her knife, and with his other hand he patted her down and ran his fingers over her other leg.

A rush of energy flowed through her. Then her body stiffened at his action. She despised it and yet liked it at the same time. Once again, Hawke was confusing her and keeping her from thinking with a rational mind. "I told ye, I dinna have any more."

"Nay?" he asked. "Well, mayhap no' on yer leg but perhaps ye're hidin' it down yer bodice." He leaned forward and glanced down her cleavage, causing her to blush. She liked the feel of his hands on her body, and also the way he was looking at her right now as if he wanted to eat her.

"Why dinna ye go ahead and check," she challenged him boldly, knowing he wouldn't do it.

"I think I will." He lifted his hand to her shoulder and let it trail down, brushing past her breast, and under her arm. She gasped. Mayhap he would do it after all! And in front of the other men no less.

His hand slid up under her breasts to the front of her causing her body to tremble. Then he leaned forward again and whispered in her ear so only she could hear him.

"One thing ye dinna ken about me is that I never back down from a challenge."

"Then ye're – ye're goin' to reach down my bodice?" she asked, her breathing labored and with a tremble to her voice. Her action only caused her chest to expand and contract more.

"Do ye want me to?" he asked, making it very tempting for her to agree.

"Do ye want me to say yes?" she asked in return, playing his game better than him.

He suddenly cleared his throat and his hand lowered from

her, settling instead on his own leg. She thought at first he wasn't feeling the same things she was experiencing right now from their little lover's game. But when he shifted in the saddle and felt something hard poking at her back, she realized he truly did want her after all. That made her smile.

"We'll continue this conversation at a later date. Come on, ye slow wenches," Hawke called back to his friends. "The last one to Elvanfoot has to hunt, make the fire, and also cook."

"What? I'm no' cookin'," complained Caleb. "I dinna cook."

"Well dinna think I'm goin' to do it," spat Logan. "That's no' my job."

"I'm the fastest rider here and ye both ken it. So I guess the two of ye are out of luck." Ethan charged off on his horse down the road in a puff of dust, leaving everyone in his wake. Logan and Caleb looked at each other and then took off at a run. Each of them urged their horse to go faster than the other's. Hawke didn't ride off, but stayed with Callum and Orrick as they drove along in the wagon.

"Are no' ye goin' to race them to camp?" asked Phoebe.

"Nay. I need to hang back and protect my great-grandda and the old sorcerer," he told her in a calm voice.

"If ye had no intention of racin' yer friends, then why did ye challenge them?" she asked in confusion.

"Just to get more time alone with ye," he whispered, his lips brushing against her ear. Her eyes closed and she tried to ignore the tingle that ran up her spine. She had to concentrate on the fact he was her enemy and she hated him. "Besides, just like me, my friends canna resist a challenge. I kent they'd fall for it. Now, they'll get there ahead of us. And they'll be so hungry and tired of waitin', that by the time we arrive, they'll have caught some game, made a fire, and cooked the food as well."

"Ye are a sneaky one, Hawke," said Callum, chuckling from the wagon, having overheard him. "I kent ye'd have somethin' up yer sleeve. Ye always have a way of gettin' others to do what ye want them to do."

"Thanks, Great-grandda. I think," said Hawke with a throaty chuckle.

Phoebe suddenly wondered what Hawke MacKeefe was trying to get her to do. She also wondered if she'd fall for it the way his friends had. If he started kissing her or running his hands up her legs again, she had a feeling her resolve wouldn't last.

CHAPTER 12

Sure enough, as Hawke planned, by the time he met up with his friends, they had a fire going and Logan was already cleaning a rabbit and a quail. Ethan busied himself constructing a spit over the fire.

"What took ye so long?" grumbled Ethan.

"We were hungry and tired of waitin' so we couldna wait any longer for ye to do it, even though ye lost the contest," added Logan.

"It smells delicious," said Hawke, coming to a stop and dismounting. "Sorry about that boys, but with the old men and the lassie along it slowed me down."

"Oh really?" asked Phoebe ignoring his proffered hand and dismounting by herself. "I thought it was all part of yer plan to get yer friends to do yer biddin'."

"It was?" Caleb looked up, polishing his sword as he sat on a rock.

"We didna slow ye down," spat Callum, climbing off the wagon. "If I wouldna had to wait for Hawke to stop three times along the way we would have been here already."

"Why did ye stop?" asked Caleb.

"He had to take a piss," grumbled Callum. "I dinna even need to stop as much and I'm a few years older than my great-grandson."

"A few?" Hawke looked over and chuckled. "And it wasna me that had to go, it was the lass."

"I'm afraid it's partially my fault," said Orrick from the bench of the wagon. "I spotted a few herbs on the way here and wanted to collect some and show them to Phoebe."

"Like I said . . . the old men and the wench slowed me down." Hawke looked up to the tree to see Apollo landing in a branch above him.

"Well, ye'd better hurry and hunt somethin' for ye and the lass to eat," said Logan, handing the rabbit and quail to Ethan to put on the spit.

"That's right," said Ethan. "It'll be dark soon."

"Oh, I see how it is," said Hawke. "I suppose ye want me to hunt for Callum and Orrick, too."

"Dinna bother," grumbled Callum. "Orrick and I have some sweetmeats and bread and plenty of Mountain Magic. We dinna need anythin' more."

"I could go for a sweetmeat. My stomach is growlin'." Hawke walked over to the wagon and reached for the bag but Callum slapped his hand away. "Nay. Ye made us put most of the provisions back, so ye'll have to find somethin' to eat on yer own."

"Well, at least give our prisoner some food," said Hawke, looking over at Phoebe.

"Nay! She's a stinkin' MacNab," Callum ground out.

"I dinna need anyone to hunt for me. Return my throwin' knife and I'll do it myself," said Phoebe.

Hawke chuckled. "Nice try, but that is no' goin' to happen. I'll hunt for both of us." He looked up at his hawk sitting in the tree. "Hunt Apollo," he commanded. The bird shrieked and took off to the sky.

"So now ye're havin' yer bird do yer biddin'?" asked Phoebe, looking at Hawke with that same disappointment in her eyes that he'd seen from his father.

"Well, if I hunt, I canna keep an eye on ye to keep ye from escapin'," he said. "If ye'd like, I can tie ye to a tree while I do it."

"I'll watch her." Caleb put down his sword and jumped to his feet. Logan and Ethan's heads both popped up.

"Nay, I'll do it," said Ethan. "I'm done here."

"Nay. She's better off with me," protested Logan. "I'm better with a sword than ye are."

"Calm down, all of ye," said Hawke. "Apollo will be back with more than enough food for everyone. In the meantime, I'll take the lass and scout the area to make sure we're no' bein' followed by the MacNabs."

"We didna see any signs of them," said Logan.

"Just because ye dinna see them doesna mean they're no' here," said Hawke, scanning his surroundings. "We canna take a chance of them sneakin' in to get the girl. I promised my da I'd find her and I did. Now we need to get her to the Highlands so I can keep my other part of the promise of protectin' my mathair and sisters and the rest of the clan."

"So that's where ye're takin' me? To the MacKeefe camp in the Highlands?" asked the girl.

"Damn," spat Hawke under his breath, not meaning to say so much in front of her. "Dinna worry where we're goin'. Now, come with me for a little ride. We're goin' on a hunt."

"Finally, ye're goin' to hunt yer own food," she remarked sarcastically.

"Nay. We're no' huntin' for food, lass. We're huntin' for MacNabs. And if there are any out there lurkin' in the shadows, ye are goin' to help me track them down."

* * *

Phoebe didn't feel comfortable at all being in the woods at

night. But with Hawke mounted on the same horse with his arm around her, she did feel safe.

"What are we lookin' for in the dark?" she asked him.

"It's no' dark yet, but it will be soon. I need to make sure no one is hidin' and waitin' to attack. Tell me about the MacNabs. Do they normally wait until a man is at a disadvantage and then kill him?"

"Nay," she said. "Just ye."

"Thanks for clarifyin' that," he answered with a puff of air from his mouth.

"Hawke, this is a waste of time. I'm sure all the MacNabs are back at the castle by now."

"I have a feelin' they might have left one or two behind to watch and see just in case we followed."

"Well, I dinna think ye're right. Can we stop at the river so I can get a drink?"

"I suppose so." After they'd dismounted, Phoebe bent down to get a drink and noticed a few wild herbs growing at the riverbank. She sat down and pulled out Orrick's book, flipping through the pages to see if she could identify them. They were losing light fast, so she had to be quick.

"So ye really want to learn to be a healer," said Hawke, hunkering down next to her.

"Of course I do. And I already am a healer or did ye forget what I did for yer wound?" She looked back at the plants and then down to the book again, still flipping through the pages.

"I didna forget. Ye have a very gentle touch and a guid way with fixin' wounds."

"Thank ye," she said, feeling a blush rise to her cheeks. She continued looking at the book rather than at him. He was close to her and his presence so near was inviting.

"Why is it so important that ye find that one weed that only grows on the Isle of Kerrera?"

"It's no' a weed. It's an herb. And there are two of them there that I need. They are powerful, healin' herbs that need to be used together. And I told ye earlier that I need it to heal someone in our clan."

"Tell me who," he challenged her, but she couldn't reveal that information.

"Ye dinna need to ken."

"It must be someone very important that ye canna get yer mind off of it."

"I think I'll just take a handful of these herbs back to camp. Then I'll be able to ask Orrick about them and also see them clearer in the firelight." She got up and stuck the book back into her pouch, bending over and picking some of the herbs. When she stood back up, something caught her eye. It was a flash of red plaid from behind a tree. She gasped.

"What is it?" Hawke drew his sword, looking around. "Did ye see someone, lass? Was it a MacNab?"

Phoebe was pretty sure she did see the MacNab plaid, but she didn't want to tell Hawke. If she did, he'd be on high alert. If one of her men was hiding in the brush as a scout like Hawke had suggested earlier, mayhap there was still hope for her to escape.

"I – I think it was an animal."

Just then, a low growl was heard and Hawke spun around with his sword in both hands and let out a low breath. "Och, it's only Jack."

"Jack?" She looked over to see Logan's wolf standing there. Ethan's wolfhound, Trapper, ran up behind it, barking. "Oh aye, it must have been him I saw."

"I think they're tryin' to get us back to camp," said Hawke. "Come on, lass. Apollo must have returned by now with some game. I'm starvin' and want to eat."

As they rode back to camp atop the horse, Phoebe looked back over her shoulder. She started wondering if she'd just imagined seeing a MacNab after all. Perhaps it was naught but wishful thinking.

* * *

"I DINNA LIKE IT," Hawke told his friends later that night after they'd eaten and were preparing to sleep. The four of them stood away from the campfire while Phoebe showed Orrick the herbs she'd collected. The two of them conversed about plants and things that Hawke didn't feel were important.

"If ye dinna like it, ye can pass the bottle of Mountain Magic over here," said Callum, grabbing it from Hawke and bringing it to his mouth.

"That's no' what I'm talkin' about, ye fool," said Hawke. "I mean I dinna like the fact that I think Phoebe saw a MacNab in the woods earlier but wouldna admit it."

"She did?" Logan's hand went to his sword, but Hawke stilled him.

"Dinna draw yer blade or she'll ken that I'm aware of it."

Ethan took the whisky from Caleb. "Do ye think there is more than one of them?" He lifted the bottle and took a swig.

"Nay. If there were more, they'd have attacked us by now," said Hawke.

"Let's go out there and find out for sure," said Logan. "I'll take Jack and search the woods."

"Jack kens he's there," said Hawke. "I'm sure that's why he growled earlier."

"Ye did, Jack?" asked Logan, looking down to his wolf. "And ye didna tear the MacNab's throat out?" The wolf was lying at Logan's feet and looked up with curious eyes.

"Stop it, Logan," said Hawke. "Ye ken our animals only attack on command. And we will no' give that command unless our lives are bein' threatened."

"Well, I for one, dinna want a MacNab sneakin' into camp while I'm sleepin' to slit my throat," said Caleb, his hand going to his neck.

"Then find a pet to alert ye and help protect ye," said Ethan.

"And no more snakes or voles," said Logan. "Make it somethin' that can put the fear into an enemy if need be."

"I'm workin' on it," said Caleb, grabbing the bottle back from Ethan. "All of ye, just leave me alone about that. I'm takin' the time to find the perfect pet."

"Hah!" spat Ethan. "By the time ye find one, we'll be auld men."

"Speakin' of auld men," said Hawke, looking back at the fire. "Keep an eye on my great-grandda. He really doesna seem to like Phoebe. And we all ken how crazy he can act once he starts drinkin' his Mountain Magic."

"He's already passed out in the back of the cart," said Ethan. "But I'll have Trapper sleep in the wagon and make sure auld Callum doesna go near Phoebe."

"I still think I should take Jack out into the forest to look for that lone MacNab," said Logan.

Hawke noticed Phoebe glance over her shoulder at them and then stand up.

"Nay, there's no need to do that," said Hawke.

"Why no'?" asked Ethan.

"Because, if there is a MacNab in the woods, he'll come to camp to get Phoebe tonight, or she'll try to sneak away to get to him. Either way, I'll be sleepin' with one eye open and will be ready for whatever happens. And this time, I swear the lass isna goin' to make me look like a fool again."

CHAPTER 13

Phoebe awakened with a jerk, startled by a noise. Realizing it was only the snoring of old Callum, she rolled onto her back, intending to go back to sleep until she saw something move in the tree above her.

At first she thought mayhap it was Hawke's bird. But then she saw the red of the MacNab plaid and knew differently. Her eyes opened wide and her heart stilled. There was her clan member, Lennox, balanced precariously on a branch above her, holding his finger to his lips to keep her from speaking and alerting the others.

She quickly glanced around the camp, but everyone was sleeping. In the light of the campfire, she saw Lennox pointing to the river.

She nodded, understanding he wanted her to meet him there. Sitting up, she silently slipped her feet into her shoes and got to her feet. Her heart raced. Lennox was here to save her and bring her back to her father! Taking one step, she realized she didn't have her bag with Orrick's book in it. Scanning the ground, she looked for it, but didn't see it. Then, she spotted it in the last place she wanted it to be. Hawke had the strap of her traveling bag over his shoulder and his hands were folded atop the bag, guarding it in his sleep. Or keeping it away from her, anyway.

She should have walked away without it, but she couldn't. Needing the knowledge written in the book to hopefully heal her father, she couldn't leave it behind. Slowly and carefully, she lifted one of Hawke's hands, moving it to the side. Then she slipped the book out from inside the bag and hurried toward the river.

HAWKE PEEKED out through slitted eyes, letting the sneaky wench think she was getting away with pulling one over on him again. His idea of sleeping with the bag instead of her tied to him worked beautifully. He knew she would never leave without Orrick's book. And in trying to sneak it away from him, she'd unknowingly woken him. He hadn't slept much all night, figuring something was going to happen, and he was right.

As soon as she left, he sat up, meaning to follow. Logan's wolf was awake and came to his side. "Let's go, Jack," he whispered. "I need yer help in trackin' down someone." He followed the wolf through the woods and toward the river.

* * *

PHOEBE HURRIED through the forest without a light to guide her. Her heart beat furiously with anxiety, excitement and hope. Now, she'd be rescued and taken back to her father. She couldn't wait. As she walked, she kept looking back over her shoulder, but couldn't see anyone following her. Then she stopped at the edge of the river and waited.

"Lennox?" she called out in a whisper. "Lennox, where are ye?" She was sure Lennox meant for her to meet him at the river, yet he was nowhere to be found. Then she heard a muffled noise, a growl, and snapping twigs. She jumped in surprise. Was there a wild animal stalking her? Bending over, she reached into her boot and pulled out her throwing knife, holding it in front of her for protection. Not sure where the noise had come from, she turned a full circle with the knife at the ready.

"Phoebe," said someone, making her spin around.

"Och, it's ye, Lennox," she said in relief, lowering her knife. "I'm glad ye're here to save me."

"Where are the MacKeefes takin' ye?" asked the man.

"We're goin' to their camp in the Highlands until the MacNabs trade their chieftain for me. Are the rest of the men already back at the castle?"

"Aye. We took The MacKeefe there and I returned as a scout. Euan figured the MacKeefes would come to the castle once he killed their messenger. The fools sent him sayin' they wanted a trade."

"Euan killed their messenger? Nay!" Phoebe's heart went out to the poor boy. "Why would my faither allow that? I think the MacNabs are the fools, no' the MacKeefes."

"Yer faither has no say anymore." Lennox spoke in a low voice, standing on the edge of the water. "He's near death and Euan has claimed the right of chieftain. He and I rule now."

"Nay," she said, not wanting to believe it. She held her body stiff and looked at him from the corner of her eye. "What did ye do with the MacKeefe laird?"

"Well, now that ye'll be back with us, Euan can either kill The MacKeefe or we can ask for a sizeable ransom. Either way, we win and the MacKeefes lose." The man actually laughed. "Let's go before those fools awake."

He turned to go, but she didn't follow. Suddenly, she didn't know if leaving was the right thing to do. She didn't want them to kill Hawke's grandfather. Neither did she want the clans to go to battle. And if Euan demanded a high ransom, the MacKeefes might not be able to pay.

"Come on, Phoebe," said Lennox, reaching out and taking her by the arm.

"Wait," she said, trying to pull loose. "Does my faither ken about all this?"

"I told ye, he has nothin' to say about it anymore. Dinna ye understand?"

She heard a sound behind her that sounded like a snarl. Lennox heard it, too, and unsheathed his sword. Then he grabbed Phoebe and held her in front of him like a shield, the coward.

"Stop right there," came a deep voice from the dark. In the light of the moon filtering through the trees, Logan's wolf and Hawke stepped out of the brush. Hawke held his sword high, ready to fight.

"Ye're goin' to have to kill us first," shouted Lennox, backing toward his horse, pulling Phoebe along with him.

"Phoebe, step away from him," commanded Hawke. "I dinna want ye stained with his bluid when I kill him."

"Nay, dinna fight! No more killin'," cried Phoebe, not knowing what to do. She didn't want Lennox to get away with this, but neither did she want Hawke killing another member of her clan. All she wanted was to go home to her father. However, she felt like she also needed Hawke's protection from Lennox and Euan now. Aye, she needed help. Her father needed help. And the worst part was, she didn't know whom to turn to in order to get it. "Hawke, just let Lennox go and I'll come back with ye, I promise. I willna give ye any trouble."

"Nay! What are ye sayin', ye fool?" cried Lennox, pulling her along with him. "Ye keep actin' like this and Euan's goin' to want to kill ye just like he did to the messenger."

"What messenger?" snapped Hawke. "And how many times do I need to tell ye to release the girl?"

"Hawke, what's goin' on?" cried one of Hawke's friends as the three men emerged from the forest.

Hawke used the distraction to his advantage. He reached

forward, pulling Phoebe away from Lennox. But when he raised his sword, Phoebe stepped back in between them with her arms spread out.

"Stay here, ye fool, I dinna care," yelled Lennox, running to his horse as Hawke's friends ran to help.

"I'll kill ye," snarled Hawke, stepping forward. But Phoebe grabbed his arm and held him back, enabling Lennox to mount his steed.

"Phoebe, stop it," spat Hawke in anger.

"I do no' want ye to kill him."

"Damn, now he's goin' to ride back to the others and they'll return with the entire clan before we get to the Highlands."

"Nay, I willna let him do that." Without thinking about it, Phoebe flung her throwing knife through the air, hitting Lennox in the shoulder. The man fell from the horse, crying out in pain.

"What . . . just happened?" asked Hawke, looking very confused.

"Hawke, we're here," said Caleb, coming to his side with Logan and Ethan. They all had their weapons drawn.

"Is it the MacNabs?" asked Logan. "I've got yer back covered."

"Calm down, it's only one," growled Hawke. "Phoebe just stopped him with a throwin' knife."

"She did what?" asked Caleb.

"Did I hear ye right?" asked Ethan. "Phoebe took down one of her own?"

"What's goin' on here?" asked Logan.

"That's what I intend to find out." Hawke stormed over to the MacNab with his sword still drawn. His friends were right on his heels.

"Who are ye and what are ye doin' here?" asked Hawke, holding his sword out to touch the man's shoulder. He moaned and tried to reach for the knife sticking out of his back.

"Phoebe, ye fool!" shouted the MacNab. "Ye'll die for what ye did."

"Dinna talk that way about the lass again or I'll kill ye where ye lay," warned Hawke. "Caleb, get his weapons. Logan, Ethan, we might have to put him out of his misery."

"Nay!" shouted Phoebe, stepping in front of Hawke with her arms stretched out. "Dinna kill Lennox. He is here alone and as a scout, that's all."

"Why shouldna I kill him?" spat Hawke. "Didna he and his friends try, and almost succeed, to do the same to me?"

"I'm only sorry ye lived," snarled the man.

"Hawke, please," begged Phoebe. "Enough killin'."

"I heard ye say he killed our messenger. Is this true?"

"It is," said Lennox. "And if ye hurt me, yer laird will die as well."

HAWKE WAS SET to slay the man, but when he heard that his grandfather's life might be in jeopardy if he killed the MacNab, he had second thoughts. Plus, Phoebe, for some reason, begged for his life. None of this made much sense.

"Tie him up," Hawke told his friends."

"What?" asked Logan, itching for a fight. "Hawke, ye're addled. Ye heard him admit he killed our messenger. That boy was innocent and didna deserve to die."

"Aye, I agree," said Hawke. "But didna ye also hear him say that our laird will be killed if anythin' happens to him?"

"He's lyin'," said Caleb. "I say we kill him."

"I agree," added Ethan.

"Nay. Please, Hawke." Phoebe's eyes met his and he couldn't bring himself to deny her request. She'd done some things tonight that he didn't understand, one of them offering to stay with him. He needed time to talk to her and to try to figure out what was going on here.

"Tie him up. He's our prisoner now," said Hawke.

"Thank ye," said Phoebe with a smile.

"And tie up the girl, too," he added.

A frown covered her face. "What?" she asked. "Hawke, what are ye doin'? I helped ye tonight."

"Ye also tried to leave, and that makes ye a traitor. If I hadna caught ye, ye'd be back at the MacNabs' castle right now. I canna let this happen again." Hawke reached down and pulled the throwing knife out of the man's shoulder. Lennox cried out in pain.

"Stop yer moanin'," said Logan, taking the man, twisting his arm behind his back.

"Come on, Phoebe," said Caleb, taking her by the arm and following Logan back to camp. The wolf went with them.

"What just happened?" Ethan asked Hawke, shaking his head.

"I'd say our little devious lassie has had a change of mind, and I dinna quite understand why," Hawke answered.

"Are we bringin' both of them back to the MacKeefe camp?" asked Ethan. "That might no' be wise since the MacNabs might storm the camp to get them back."

"I'm no' sure what we're goin' to do." Hawke looked over to the MacNab's horse, realizing it was his. "Welcome back, guid friend," he said, heading over and grabbing the reins of his horse that they'd stolen from him. It felt good to have his steed back, but it felt bad to think he was going to have to trade Phoebe for his grandfather. He didn't really want her to go.

As he looked down to the bloody throwing knife in his hand, he smiled. The wench always had something up her sleeve, down her bodice, or tucked inside her boot, it seemed. Aye, he was going to miss the little spitfire, but he had no choice but to trade her back to the MacNabs in exchange for his grandfather. Then another idea lodged in his brain of how to do it, but it was crazy. Then again, a crazy stunt like this might get him a mention in that damned book of the Highland Chronicles if he managed to pull it off and not get killed.

CHAPTER 14

"Hold still and let me tend to yer wounds. Both of ye," said Phoebe the next morning. Hawke sat shirtless on a log and Lennox was next to him, also shirtless but with his hands tied together in front of him.

"Phoebe, my wound is healed," Hawke told her impatiently. He didn't want to sit next to the man who'd been involved in almost killing him, slaying some of the MacKeefes, and abducting his grandfather.

Phoebe worked on Lennox, and that bothered him that she saw to his needs first. "I've got things to do and we need to be on our way." Hawke stood up, letting every little thing bother him this morning.

"Wait. Let me see yer wound." Phoebe reached over and gently touched his shoulder. "I canna believe it. It is just about healed. These herbal creams work better than I thought." She rubbed some on his shoulder anyway, causing a flitting feeling to wash through him. With her standing so close to him, he could smell her womanly scent that reminded him of a field of heather. He had to get away from her because he was starting to want to kiss her again.

"That's enough," he commanded, stepping away from her and donning his tunic. "Clean up and break down camp, everyone. We've got to take to the road," he called out.

"I'm no' finished yet," complained Phoebe.

"I say ye are."

"Nay, I'm no' done dressin' Lennox's wound."

"Let Orrick do it. Phoebe, I need to speak to ye in private."

"But –"

"Now."

"I'll tend to his wound," offered Orrick, hurrying over to help Lennox.

"Let the cur die," called out old Callum from the wagon. "He has my son and willna get away with it."

"Callum, have a little more Mountain Magic while ye're waitin'," said Hawke, hoping to calm down his great-grandfather before he did something stupid. Hawke took Phoebe by the arm and pulled her to the side.

"What do ye want?" she asked, wiping the cream off her hands with a cloth.

"We need to talk."

"Hawke, I already told ye. I'm sorry I tried to escape again, but I wanted to get back to my faither."

"That's no' what I wanted to talk to ye about."

"It isna?" Her eyes rose to his and then trailed back down. "Then what?"

"I want to ken why ye flung yer knife at Lennox – one of yer own men, last night."

"I did it because I wanted to stop him. If he made it back to Crookston Castle, he'd return here with more MacNabs just like ye said. I didna want to see ye and the others dyin' before my very eyes."

"I dinna believe ye."

"What?" She looked up at him and her brows dipped. "Why no'?"

"Phoebe, I think there is somethin' ye are no' tellin' me. Does it have to do with yer faither?"

"I dinna ken what ye mean."

"Is yer da the one who is ailin'?"

"Nay, of course no'," she said. "My faither is a strong chieftain."

"I heard Lennox tell ye that yer faither has nothin' to say about things anymore. Why no'?"

"All right, I admit my faither is ill," she answered with a sigh. "But he's still the laird and makes all the decisions."

"So it was his choice to kill our messenger who came in peace with a letter askin' for a trade?"

"Nay, that was of Euan's doin'. My faither, I am sure, wants peace between our clans."

"Ye'd better hope that's the case. Because if no', I swear I will do whatever I have to in order to rescue my grandfaither."

"Dinna worry. I'm sure my faither will trade yer grandfaither for me."

"And what about him?" asked Hawke, nodding toward Lennox. "Will he want him as well?"

"Aye," she said, not sounding so certain. Hawke had a feeling she answered that way just so he wouldn't think of the man as worthless extra baggage, and kill him before they got to the Highlands.

"Hawke, we've got the prisoner tied up and in the cart," called out Logan. "We're ready to go. Do ye want the girl tied up and in the back of the wagon as well?"

Phoebe's eyes darted up to his and she looked panicked. "Hawke, ye dinna need to tie me up."

"Why no'? Ye're a prisoner, the same as he."

"I'm ready," said Caleb, walking past with something in his arms.

"Wait, Caleb," said Hawke, stopping him. "What have ye got there?"

"It's my new pet," he answered, holding up a long animal with a black and cream-colored striped face. "I found her down at the riverbed."

"That's a polecat!" spat Hawke in surprise. "Get rid of it. Fast!"

"Nay," protested Phoebe. "I think it's kind of cute."

"Believe me, they dinna make guid pets," Hawke assured her.

"I like it." Phoebe reached out to pet it. The animal opened its mouth showing fangs, and lifted one paw with sharp claws, scratching her.

"Och!" Phoebe screamed, jumping back, startling the animal.

"Nay! Dinna startle it." Hawke grabbed her and pulled her into his arms, turning them both around, making distance between them and Caleb.

"Oh, hell!" Caleb grumbled, as the air was filled with a pungent stench.

"Now do ye see what I mean?" asked Hawke.

"I'll get rid of it," said Caleb, sounding disheartened, heading away.

"Take a jump in the river while ye're there," Hawke called after him. "Ye stink!"

Ten minutes later, Caleb returned, dripping wet. Everyone was ready to leave.

"Egads, boy, I can smell ye all the way from here," complained Callum from the wagon. "That stench will alert any enemy from here to the Highlands that we're comin'."

"It'll take a while to rid yerself of the smell," Hawke told him.

"Well, ye willna be takin' any lassies to yer bed, that's for sure," said Ethan, causing both him and Logan to burst out laughing.

"Callum's right. We'll no' be able to sneak up on the enemy with ye around," said Logan.

"Let's go," Callum shouted from the wagon. "I need to get back to the Horn and Hoof. We're almost out of Mountain Magic."

"Give me some whisky," complained Lennox from the back of the cart. "And get me out of this wagon."

Lennox had been causing so much trouble, that they'd had to tie both his hands and legs together and then tie him to the wagon as well.

"I'll no' waste guid whisky on the likes of ye," growled Callum, leaning over and spitting over the side of the wagon from the front bench seat.

"It might help with the pain from his wound," suggested Orrick. "Mayhap we should give him some after all. His wound is starting to fester."

"It's fine. Let him have it," said Hawke.

"But didna ye hear Callum?" asked Ethan. "We're almost out of Mountain Magic."

"Give him the rest," Hawke said once again, knowing the greedy man would guzzle it down and pass out at least until they got to Glasgow. It was what he wanted – peace and quiet.

"Here, ye bluidthirsty, no guid MacNab." Callum threw him the bottle and Lennox caught it with his tied hands.

"Ye'd better tie her up and get her in the cart, too." Logan told Hawke, speaking of Phoebe.

Phoebe's head snapped around and her eyes met Hawke's once again in a silent, desperate plea. Hawke didn't have the heart to tie her up and he certainly didn't want to put her next to Lennox. There was no telling what that man might do to her.

"Nay, she'll ride with me."

"Ye want this?" Ethan offered him some rope.

"There's no need," Hawke answered. "She's no' goin' anywhere as long as she's with me." He reached over and hoisted Phoebe up onto his horse and pulled himself up behind her.

It was all worth it when she looked over her shoulder and smiled at him, her face lighting up. She looked like an angel. Then she whispered, "Thank ye, Hawke." Having the enemy thank him wasn't a normal thing to happen. But coming from a bonnie wench like her, he liked it. Hawke was starting to have feelings for Phoebe. He struggled inwardly with the fact that he was going to have to trade her back to the MacNabs if he ever wanted to see his grandfather again.

"We ride to Glasgow," Hawke commanded, without answering her. Once she found out what he planned to do when they got there, she might not be so eager to thank him again.

* * *

PHOEBE HAD a feeling something was troubling Hawke. More so than usual, anyway. They'd ridden for hours and he hadn't said more than a few words to her the entire time. And when she purposely asked him a question, trying to get him to speak, he only answered with a grunt.

Finally, the Horn and Hoof Tavern came into view and the traveling party stopped.

"It's guid to be back," said Callum with a huge smile, almost jumping from the wagon in anticipation to get back to the tavern he owned. Callum rushed inside while Orrick went to the back of the cart to check on their prisoner.

"He's sleeping like a babe," said Orrick, checking the man's shoulder. "But I don't like the looks of his wound. I'm going to need more herbs to rid him of that infection."

"Let him die. He deserves it," said Caleb, walking by. The smell of the polecat still clung to him and Phoebe had to cover her nose with her hand. "Let's go inside and get a drink."

"Nay, ye're no' goin' to sully the Horn and Hoof with yer stench." Hawke slipped off the horse and reached up and put his hands on Phoebe's waist to help her dismount. She held on to his broad shoulders as he lifted her and slid her down his body.

Being so close, with their bodies touching, it made Phoebe feel warm and excited.

"What do ye mean?" complained Caleb. "I'm no' stayin' out here."

"Aye, ye are," said Hawke. "Stay in the barn with the horses tonight and I'll have someone bring ye some food and ale later."

"Nay," Caleb said with a scowl. "I'm goin' in to find somethin' to eat." Caleb took two steps before he was blocked by Ethan.

"I agree with Hawke. No one in there wants to smell yer stench." Ethan crossed his arms over his chest.

"Get outta my way, Ethan!" Caleb sidestepped Ethan, only to be stopped by Logan blocking his path next.

"I'll use brute force to keep ye here if I have to," Logan warned him, his arms crossing over his chest as well.

"Ye canna keep me outta the tavern," Caleb spat.

"Fine, let him pass then, boys," said Hawke, releasing Phoebe. "But I'll hate to see what my great-grandda does to him if he dares to step a foot inside the tavern reekin' like dung."

"That's right," said Logan. "The last time I walked into the Horn and Hoof with just mud from the road on my feet, old Callum had the bouncers throw me out on my ear."

"That's nothin'," said Ethan. "Callum didna like the fact I had my elbows on the drink bar one day and he actually stabbed my hand with a knife. Dinna ye remember?"

"Och, that's right," said Caleb, making a face and looking at the ground. "Ye bled all over me since I was sittin' next to ye at the time."

"Boys, haul the prisoner into the barn as well and make sure he canna escape," said Hawke. "Caleb, ye watch him until we decide what to do with him."

"Me?" Caleb's palm slapped against his chest. "I dinna want to watch a stinkin' MacNab. He's likely to find a way to get loose and slit my throat as I sleep."

Phoebe stirred restlessly, not liking that he was insinuating all MacNabs were like Lennox.

"I find it amusin' ye use the word stinkin'," said Hawke with a chuckle. "So dinna sleep, then, I dinna care," said Hawke, throwing the travel bag from the horse over his shoulder and taking Phoebe by the arm. "Come on, lass. We're gettin' a room for the night."

"A room?" asked Ethan. "Oh, guid. I'd like to sleep on a pallet tonight instead of the ground."

"The room is no' for any of ye. I'll be watchin' the lass, but it'll just be the two of us," Hawke informed his friends.

"Nay, I willna stay in a room with ye," protested Phoebe. "It wouldna be right. I'm a woman and ye're a man."

"Very guid," said Hawke with a wry smile. "I'm glad ye noticed."

"That's no' what I mean. I mean . . . it wouldna be proper."

"Would ye rather stay out in the barn with Caleb and Lennox? Because I can arrange that," Hawke told her.

Phoebe's stomach was already turning from the smell of the polecat. Plus, she didn't want to be anywhere near that cur, Lennox. "Nay, I'll stay with ye in the room," she finally agreed, since it was the lesser of two evils.

"Now that it's settled, let's get inside and have ourselves some food and ale."

"Hell with the ale," said Logan, making a beeline for the tavern. "I want some Mountain Magic."

"Nay, none of that tonight," Hawke told him. "We need to stay alert. We've got a job to do."

"A job? What job?" asked Phoebe.

"Never ye mind," grumbled Hawke, pulling Phoebe into the tavern with him.

"A h'ay penny to enter," said the bouncer at the door. He was a burly Scot that kept the customers in line. By charging money to enter, it assured there would be enough funds to fix any damage done by unruly men who became drunk.

"Hello, Albert," said Hawke, knowing the man.

"Hawke." The large man smiled and nodded. "I dinna realize

at first it was ye. It's been a while since ye've been here. But who is the lass?"

"She's no one," Hawke answered, making Phoebe angry.

"No one? I'm Phoebe Mac–"

She was cut off by Hawke's mouth closing down on hers. Suddenly, she forgot about everything except Hawke's lips caressing her mouth. She went weak in the knees from such a strong, powerful kiss from this admirable warrior.

"Oh, she's yer wench," said Albert with a nod and a grin. "I understand. Go on in, Hawke. Ye ken there is no charge for Callum's family and their doxies."

"What did ye call me?" asked Phoebe, shocked by the man's accusation.

"Here's a coin for yer trouble," said Hawke, handing one to the man anyway. By habit, the man bounced the coin on the wet board he held to make sure it was real. Hawke pulled Phoebe along with him as he headed inside the tavern.

"I dinna like what he said about me," sniffed Phoebe, looking over her shoulder. "Why didna ye tell him the truth about who I am?"

"Ye do that, and every enemy of the MacNabs inside here will be out for bluid," Hawke explained. "It's best not to let them ken ye're a MacNab. That's the reason I didna want Lennox inside."

"Oh," she said with nod. "So is that also why ye kissed me? Just so I wouldna tell anyone who I was?"

"Nay, Phoebe," said Hawke, stopping and lifting her chin with two fingers, looking deep into her eyes. "I kissed ye because I wanted to."

"Ye lie." Her jaw clenched in aggravation. "I dinna like when ye play yer silly games."

"It's no' a game," he told her.

She glared at him, knowing better.

"Oh, all right, mayhap that was why I kissed ye. But I also wanted to kiss ye again just because I enjoyed it the first time."

"I dinna believe ye did."

"What do I have to do to prove to ye that I like kissin' ye and bein' with ye? And ye canna tell me that ye dinna like the kiss because I saw how ye clung to me and yer legs quivered beneath ye."

"I'm yer enemy, Hawke," she reminded him. "We both ken that after the exchange between the clans, we'll never see each other again. Therefore, I dinna think it matters what either of us feels. It was a mistake and I willna allow it to happen again. All I want is to get back to my faither."

"Well, that might be happenin' sooner than ye think," Hawke mumbled, walking to a table and plopping his travel bag down upon it.

"What do ye mean?" She hurried to join him.

"Dinna worry yer pretty little head about a thing, lass." Hawke reached out and lifted her chin again, running his thumb over her bottom lip as his gaze focused once more on her mouth.

"Dinna touch me," she said, pushing away his hand.

"Stop it," he whispered. "People are startin' to stare. We dinna want them to think we're anythin' but lovers. If so, they are goin' to start askin' questions that I am no' willin' to answer. Now sit down and I'll get us somethin' to eat."

Phoebe collapsed atop the bench, noticing everyone staring at her. Men with their hands cradled around metal tankards talked and laughed. Some of them had whores on their laps. The girls wore low-cut bodices and pressed their cleavages up against the men's cheeks.

"Lovers," she said to herself, clutching her cloak to her neck, watching the local lightskirts working the room. Everyone seemed to be happy and enjoying themselves. Everyone but her. Phoebe felt so alone right now.

The man at the door thought she was Hawke's lover. What if she truly were Hawke's lover? The idea excited her at first, but then she let out a sigh realizing it could never happen. Being enemies, all she was to Hawke was a means to get his grandfather returned. Nothing more. But if things had been different, she wondered if perhaps she and Hawke could have been lovers after all.

CHAPTER 15

"Ye're addled, Hawke," said Logan, taking a swig of ale. Logan, Ethan, and Hawke stood outside the door to the room that Hawke was sharing with Phoebe.

"It's a suicide mission," added Ethan, leaning against the wall.

"Shhh," said Hawke, looking over to the door. "I dinna want Phoebe to hear us."

"Ye canna rescue Ian by yerself," said Logan. "That is out of the question."

"At least take us with ye," said Ethan. "And Caleb, too."

"Nay," said Hawke. "They'd smell Caleb comin'." He flashed his friends a smile, trying to keep the mood light.

"Why dinna ye just wait until we get to the MacKeefe camp?" Ethan stifled a yawn.

"Because, I dinna want to bring our prisoners into the camp with our women and children present. It's too dangerous."

"No' any more dangerous than ye tryin' to sneak in and break yer grandfaither out of the dungeon all by yerself," said Logan. "Ye could get killed, or even taken prisoner yerself."

"Dinna worry about it. If that happens, we still have two prisoners to trade for Ian and me." All of a sudden, Hawke smelled something foul and looked up to see Caleb approaching. "Caleb, I thought I told ye to stay in the barn and watch the prisoner," said Hawke.

"Jack and Trapper are watchin' him. Plus Orrick was headed out to the barn as well. I came in to get a bath. I willna be shunned any longer while ye three have all the fun."

"Hah!" spat Ethan. "If ye call a suicide mission fun."

"What do ye mean?" asked Caleb. "What's goin' on?"

"Hawke is goin' to sneak into the MacNab camp tonight and try to break out his grandda," Logan told him.

"Why?" Caleb turned his head and looked at Hawke from the corner of his eye. "Is this an attempt to get mentioned in the Highland Chronicles? Because if so . . . I like it." He smiled and nodded his approval.

"Ye're both daft," said Ethan with a wave of his hand through the air. "No book is that important to take on a mission that is sure to fail."

"I dinna care about the Highland Chronicles, and I willna fail," said Hawke. "I care about my grandda and the clan. This feud has gone on long enough and no more MacKeefes are goin' to die. Since they killed our messenger, that tells me they are no' willin' to negotiate. When my faither finds out, he'll want to attack. It'll be a bluidy battle and many will die. I need to end this now before it is too late."

"I suppose ye're right," said Ethan.

"Has anyone heard more news about the attack from the English?"

"I heard they are movin' up the coast," said Caleb. "A traveler passin' by told me out in the barn that the Scots are still burnin' the land but holdin' off on fightin'. They're plannin' to ambush the English as soon as they move north. Hopefully, the English will turn around and go home."

"With the forces split, hopefully the MacNabs' defenses at their castle will be weaker," said Hawke.

"How do ye plan on gettin' in and out without bein' seen?" asked Logan. "We dinna ken anythin' about Crookston Castle."

"Mayhap no'," said Hawke, looking at the door to his room. "But I ken someone who does."

"Ye think Phoebe is goin' to tell ye how to sneak into her castle?" asked Ethan.

"No' willingly. But I think I can get her to spill their secrets, like where to find their hidden postern gate."

"Be careful, Hawke," said Ethan. "Ye dinna want to play that game. No' if ye care about the lass at all."

"We're enemies," Hawke reminded him. "Whatever I feel doesna matter because when I'm through, we'll have our chieftain back and Phoebe will be back where she belongs."

"And what about Lennox?" asked Caleb. "What are ye plannin' to do with him?"

"We'll keep him as a backup plan for now. But honestly, I dinna care if the man lives or dies after what he's done."

* * *

PHOEBE PRESSED her ear to door, having heard every word of Hawke's ill-conceived plan. How dare he think he could use her to get information to work against her clan? Well, two could play this game. She'd let Hawke think he was winning but, in reality, she would be the victor in the end.

The door latch moved and she hurried back to the other side of the room. Hawke walked in with a bottle of wine in one hand and two wooden goblets in the other.

"Phoebe," he said. "I thought ye'd be sleepin' by now."

"Nay," she said, staring out the open window. "I dinna plan on sleepin' at all tonight."

"Why no'?" He closed and locked the door, and headed across the room.

"Because," she said, holding her tongue and trying not to spill her secret that she knew his plan.

"Ye look upset. Is somethin' botherin' ye?"

She eyed the vines climbing up to the second floor room wondering if they'd hold her weight. Either way, she supposed it didn't matter. She'd never be able to sneak out if Hawke was there. She'd have to wait until he fell asleep, or mayhap she'd have to pretend to sleep and wait until he left the room first.

"Nay, no' at all," she said, faking a smile.

"Well, let's have some wine and relax." He reached over and closed the shutter, leaving her trapped in the room alone with him. If she hadn't overheard his plan, she might like sharing some wine and perhaps a few kisses. But now, she trusted him even less than she had before. She needed to be careful not to tell him any real information that he could use to his advantage.

"All right," she said, her arms crossed over her chest.

"Come, and sit down," he told her, putting the wine on the table and sitting on the bed.

She hesitated, but then did as he asked. He poured out two cups of wine and handed one to her. "Tell me about your clan."

"There's nothin' to tell. Ye and I are enemies." She took a sip of wine.

"Well, it doesna have to stay that way." He reached over and put his arm around her. She stiffened. And when he leaned over to kiss her, she turned her head. She'd meant to lead him on, but she just couldn't do it. "Have some more wine, Phoebe."

She downed the white wine and got up and paced the floor. "Hawke, I'm no' goin' to tell ye anythin' so dinna bother tryin'."

"I see." He looked into his cup swirling the contents. "I think I need somethin' stronger than wine." He got up and walked across the room, tapping the floor with his foot. The candlelight lit the room dimly, but she could tell he was looking for something.

"What are ye doin'?" she asked.

"I ken my great-grandda always has a little Mountain Magic

stashed away in each of these rooms. He hides it everywhere, never wanting to run out." He bent down and yanked away a loose board. "Ah, here it is." Reaching down into the floor, he pulled out a bottle. Then getting up, he brought it over to the bed. Using his teeth, he uncorked the bottle, poured some into her cup, and held it out to her, resting his hand on her shoulder.

"I dinna care for any." She pushed his hand off of her and looked the other way.

"Phoebe, I dinna like to see ye so tense. Just have a sip to relax. Ye're actin' like a frigid nun."

"I am no' actin' like a nun!" She didn't like to be called a doxie by the doorman and neither did she like being called a nun by him. Mayhap a drink would help since, right now, she felt like she was going to cry. She didn't like being a prisoner and being kept away from her ailing father. Perhaps if she convinced him to drink the Mountain Magic as well, he'd pass out and then she'd be able to escape. Then she'd head to the MacNab territory that wasn't far from here. "I'll drink some if ye do as well."

He looked at the cup as if he were considering it and then raised it to his lips. Her eyes fastened to his throat as he drank it down as if it were naught but water. Then he pressed his lips together, closed his eyes partially and let out a satisfied sigh. "It only gets better with age," he said, filling up the cup again and handing it to her. "Go ahead. Try it."

"I will." She grabbed the cup and took a small sip and tried to hand it back. He looked at her and chuckled. Kicking off his boots, he proceeded to remove his weapon belt. "What's so funny?" she asked.

"I can tell ye're a MacNab because ye're afraid."

"I'm no' afraid of ye." She watched as he removed his tunic next. Her eyes settled on his wide and sturdy naked chest.

"I didna mean me, lass. I meant ye're afraid of the Mountain Magic."

"I'm no' afraid of it. I'm just no' thirsty. Besides, it is no' a drink for ladies."

"I beg to differ." He plopped down on the bed and stretched his legs out in front of him. "Caleb's mathair, Kyla, is a little thing yet she can outdrink most of the men when it comes to Mountain Magic. I've never seen anythin' like it. She is a remarkable woman and one of a kind."

"I could drink it, too, if I wanted."

"Dinna let me stop ye, lass." He smiled at her, making her heart flutter as he held out the cup, lounging back on the bed. Hawke's naked chest called to her and his smile made her heart flutter. "Come," he coaxed her, letting his eyes sweep down her body. "Sit on the bed with me, Phoebe. I promise I willna bite."

She stared at him a moment, then slowly uncrossed her arms and let them drop to her sides. "All right," she answered in a soft whisper, padding across the room and reaching out for the cup. Her eyes interlocked with his as she raised the goblet to her mouth in an attempt to prove to him that she could be a remarkable, one-of-a-kind woman as well. She only took two swallows, but it was enough to make her choke since the whisky was so strong. She put the cup on the bedside table, coughing and clutching her throat with one hand.

"Lass, are ye all right?" he asked with a chuckle, sitting up and pulling her into his arms. Feeling lightheaded from the whisky, his action set her off balance. She leaned up against him, both of them falling back on the bed. In a prone position atop Hawke, Phoebe's body pressed against his.

"I like this," he whispered, reaching up and untying the ribbon from her hair, letting it fall loose around her shoulders. "Ye are a bonnie lass." His fingers grazed the side of her cheek and Phoebe found herself lost in the depths of his bright blue eyes. Hawke looked even more handsome up close. And when he gently pulled her head toward him and lifted his chin, her eyes closed as their lips touched. A delicious shiver swept through her.

"So do I," she admitted, sighing and rolling off his chest, lying on the bed next to him on her back.

"Have some more Mountain Magic," he said, handing her the cup. "And tell me about yerself."

She had wanted to trick him, seduce him, and play the game better than he. But with one more sip of the whisky, the tone of his voice started to sound as if he really cared. Instead of trying to deceive him, she found herself opening up to him.

"My mathair died six years ago, birthin' my little brathair, Miles. I was Lady of the Castle then and raised him as if I were his mathair."

"Oh, I'm sorry." They sat up next to each other drinking the whisky with their backs propped against the headboard. "Do ye have other siblin's?"

She nodded. "I am the oldest, but my sister, Elspeth is fourteen and Agan is only ten. Do ye have siblin's, too?"

"Well," he said, pouring himself another cup of the golden liquid. "I do. My faither, as ye already ken, is Storm MacKeefe. My mathair's name is Wren. She is an English noble. Renard is my older half-brathair. I also have an older sister named Lark, and a younger sister, Heather."

"Ye are a guid warrior, Hawke. Did ye learn how to fight from yer faither?"

"And my grandda," said Hawke. "Where did ye learn to throw knives? Ye are a pretty guid aim."

"Thank ye. I learned on my own. I did it for protection. No' only mine, but also that of my siblin's."

"How often do ye use it?" he asked.

"Only when I have to," she answered. "I was attacked once by a man who wanted to use me for his pleasures. I was on the road alone, collectin' herbs in a storm. An illness was sweepin' through our clan and I wanted to heal everyone."

"What happened to yer attacker?" asked Hawke.

"I – I killed him," she said, feeling full of remorse. I didna mean to do it, but my blade went right through his heart." Phoebe didn't like the way it felt to take a life, even if it was a roadside bandit.

"Come here, lass," he said, pulling her into his arms.

"Does it ever get any easier?" she asked.

"To kill?"

"Aye."

"Nay. It never feels guid to take a life," he told her. "But I try no' to focus on that. I try, instead, to pay more attention to all the lives I've saved."

"Hawke, I'm frightened for my faither. If what Lennox says is true, then I fear he really has lost control, just like ye suspected. He is ill and needs me to heal him. I dinna even ken if Euan has hurt him or possibly killed him by now." A tear involuntarily slipped from her eye. Hawke reached out and brushed it away with his thumb.

"Dinna think of that tonight, lass. Instead, only think of the time we are spendin' together, in case it never happens again."

"And why would that be?" she asked, waiting for him to tell her the truth that on his mission to Crookston Castle he might be killed.

He didn't answer her, and neither did he ask any more questions. Instead, he reached over and put both arms around her, kissing her deeply and letting his tongue enter her mouth.

Something within her made her forget he was the enemy. Instead, she focused on what she had tonight, hoping it would turn into more than just kisses. Then his open hands slid higher, up her sides, brushing against her breasts. He continued his exploration by pushing her bodice off her shoulders and nuzzling her neck. Her breathing labored as his face came closer to her cleavage.

"I canna get enough of ye, lass," he whispered, his breath on her skin feeling hot and sultry. It caused her to be filled with lust. And when he reached up and slid the fingers of one hand beneath her bodice, cupping her bare breast, her head fell back with her eyes closed.

His thumb brushed past her nipple once, and then twice, causing it to go taut in anticipation. Rolling the nub between his fingers, she felt the excitement within her growing and tingling all the way down between her legs.

His mouth replaced his hand and his tongue swirled around her nipple. Then his free hand caressed her twin peak. Suckling at her, he removed his breeches with his other hand. When she realized what he was doing, she glanced downward, seeing his erection and gasped.

"Hawke, mayhap we should slow down," she said, suddenly feeling frightened.

"I will try, but ye have me so hot and bothered right now, love, that if I do no' take ye, I swear I'm goin' to burst."

"I dinna think –"

"Feel," he said, taking her hand and wrapping it around his hardened form. She gasped again at the size of this lusty warrior, wondering how it would feel for him to enter her. She meant to pull away but now she was so randy that she squirmed beneath him on the bed. And when he pushed up her gown and pulled off her braies, she felt as if she could barely wait. He cupped her mound and caressed her womanly folds. Guided by her own liquid passion, his finger slid forward, entering her. Moaning in pleasure, she had all she could do not to lift her legs and wrap them around him. She needed to feel him inside her. She wanted him even closer. Aye, she felt the urgency and desire to have him!

Mayhap it was the whisky controlling her actions, or perhaps only her unsated lust that made her do it. But she felt so randy that she wasn't about to let him pull away.

"Take me, Hawke. Make love to me. I want to ken how it feels to be yer lover."

"Och, lass, ye make it hard to say nay."

"I willna let ye leave, so dinna even try." With that, she

managed to raise her legs around his waist, hearing a low moan at the back of his throat.

"Are ye sure, love?" he asked, hesitating. She saw the need in his eyes. "After all, we are enemies."

"Do ye find it excitin' to think about beddin' yer enemy?" she asked.

"I find it excitin' to think about beddin' ye."

"I have never wanted a man the way I do ye," she said. "Do, it, Hawke. Do it, before one of us pulls away and leaves us both unfulfilled and unsated."

He slid his manhood into her, slowly at first almost as if he were teasing her. She clamped her legs around him tighter. "I want more," she cried. "More. Please."

"I canna deny a lassie when she says please."

He thrust his full length into her then, and she stiffened just for a moment to get used to his size. He slid out and back in and their rhythm became faster and faster. Her back arched up off the bed.

Then he grabbed her buttocks in his hands and lifted her, getting to his knees.

"What are ye doin'?" she asked.

"I always wanted to try it standin' up."

"I dinna think that's possible."

"Do ye want to find out?"

Excitement grew within her. "Aye," she answered with a giggle.

In a moment, he had her off the bed and she clung to him with her legs spread, gripping him around his waist. With her hands on his shoulders, she helped in the dance of love, moving up and down on his slick shaft, both of them moaning in delight.

"Och, lassie, ye are drivin' me from my mind." His tongue shot out and he managed to lick her cleavage. Then he had her back up against the wall as he thrust into her again, making her cry out in elation as she reached her peak, no longer able to hold back.

"Are ye sated?" he asked, breathing heavy, holding off until he knew she'd found her release.

"Oh, yes," she said, barely able to breathe.

"Guid," he answered, taking her back to the bed, lying down with her on top of him, never breaking the connection.

"What are ye doin', Hawke?"

"I want ye to do it again," he said, sounding as if he were going to explode.

"What do ye mean? Find my release again?"

"Aye."

"That isna possible."

"Och, yes it is, lass. Let me help ye."

He reached up and pulled at her nipple with his lips, slightly grazing her with his teeth. Then, holding her hips he squeezed her back end, he pumped into her, making her come to life all over again.

"Oooh," she moaned, feeling her body responding to his advances. Then he hit a spot she didn't know existed and it felt so good that she cried out loudly. It was more like a scream. "Oooh, Hawke!"

"That's what I wanted to hear," he told her, this time rolling atop her and continuing to make love until he filled her with his seed of life.

Both of them hot, wet, and sated, they collapsed atop the bed, holding each other, trying to regain their breathing.

"That was . . . amazin'," she said.

"Ye are amazin'," he replied. "I didna mean for that to happen, lass."

"Neither did I. But I suppose now, we're really lovers."

"Aye. Enemies and lovers," he said, closing his eyes and falling asleep.

Phoebe didn't expect him to say that. After their intimate time together, she didn't think he'd still consider her the enemy. If she wasn't so tired from making love and so lightheaded from the Mountain Magic, mayhap she could have thought of escaping. But instead, she leaned her head on Hawke's chest and went to sleep.

CHAPTER 16

Hawke stirred restlessly in his sleep as his nightmare once more returned.

"Osla, ye stay here while I go after the deer," said Hawke, taking an arrow from his quiver and moving forward on his horse through the woods. Hawke's skill with the sword was phenomenal, but he only used the bow and arrows to hunt.

This was the first time Hawke went on the hunt with the MacNabs since he married Osla MacNab to make an alliance with the MacKeefes' enemy. Osla lived with the MacKeefes and Hawke didn't know many of the men from her clan, nor did he want to.

Angus MacNab was their chieftain and he was on the hunt as well. He lined up the shot, but when a MacNab came bounding through the forest on his horse, the deer doubled back the way they'd come.

"There it goes," said the MacNab. "Shoot it, fast, before it gets away."

"It's too far," he said, but the MacNab wouldn't let up.

"Do it, if ye want to gain favors in our chieftain's eyes."

Hawke wanted this alliance between the clans to go well. For seven months now he'd been married to Osla and he still felt like an outsider around the MacNabs. He didn't love Osla and she seemed to have no desire to be with him. Still, he was her husband and her protector.

Hawke shot the arrow, but as he let it loose, the MacNab's horse reared up.

"Damn!" Hawke spat as the arrow shot off through the forest. "Why did ye do that?"

"The horse became skittish, I canna help it," said the man.

Hawke rode back to Osla, but when he approached the place that he left her, she wasn't there. Instead, the MacNabs were gathered around the edge of a steep drop off, looking down.

"What is goin' on?" asked Hawke as he dismounted and walked to the edge of the drop of. "Where is Osla?"

"She's there," said their chieftain, pointing down the cliff. Hawke's body stiffened as he looked down to see Osla lying face down on the ground with an arrow sticking out of her back. Her gown was soaked in blood. "The men tell me a stray arrow struck her and her horse reared up, throwing her off, down the steep rocks."

"Osla!" he shouted, rushing down the rocks where another MacNab was leaning over her.

The man looked up and shook his head. "She's dead," he said.

"Nay!" Hawke shook his head and rushed forward, but another MacNab held him back. "Stay away from her," snapped the one hunkered over her body.

"Isna that Hawke's arrow in her back?" It was the man whose horse reared up and caused him to miss his mark.

"It is," said the man on the ground, pulling it from Osla's back and holding it up high. "Hawke MacKeefe killed his own wife."

"Nay, I didna," he shouted, trying once again to get to Osla, but now three MacNabs held him back. Then the chieftain came down the hill to join them.

"Hawke MacKeefe, we had an alliance, yet ye killed a MacNab," said Angus MacNab.

"It was an accident," he said, shaking his head, not wanting to believe his wife was dead. "I dinna ken how it happened, but I didna mean to do it."

"He's our enemy," said one of the MacNabs.

"He broke the alliance," said another.

Hawke drew his sword, ready to fight them all if need be. They closed in around him with eyes of fire.

"Nay," said Angus, holding his hand in the air. "We will no' kill him now. But he will go back to his clan and tell them that the feud between the MacNabs and the MacKeefes is no' over. Now, it is goin' to be even a worse feud than before."

"Nay!" Hawke cried, as a fog surrounded him. "Nay, this canna be happenin'."

Hawke awoke in a cold sweat, realizing it was just his nightmare again. But what happened was real and something he could never forget. If he hadn't left Osla to hunt a deer and had been with her instead to protect her, none of this would have ever happened. He thought of the man whose horse reared up and then he thought of the one hunkering down over the body of his dead wife. It was ten long years ago and he hadn't known the MacNabs, but a realization hit him hard.

He sat up in bed, seeing Phoebe sleeping soundly next to him. Looking toward the window, he realized it was close to daybreak. He'd never meant to fall asleep. But after the wonderful night of making love with Phoebe, it left him exhausted.

Hawke dressed and snuck out of the room, making his way to the stable.

"Where've ye been, Hawke?" Caleb was in the stable, no longer stinking if Hawke wasn't mistaken. Lennox lay in the hay with his arms and legs still tied and Orrick was checking his wound. "It's almost daybreak. I thought ye were goin' to sneak into the MacNab's castle durin' the night."

Hawke noticed both Lennox and Orrick look up when he said that.

"Haud yer wheesht, Caleb." Looking down at Lennox, it was clear to him now. Lennox and Euan were the men from his dream. They were the ones he didn't know ten years ago – the ones he was sure framed him somehow. He didn't know how they did it, since it was his arrow in Osla's back, but he was sure they were the ones to kill her, not him. Now, he just had to prove it. He walked over to Lennox, wanting to kill him right there. But if he were to prove his innocence, he'd need the man alive. "Ye framed me, I ken it."

"I dinna ken what ye're talkin' about," said Lennox.

"It bothered me for ten years that I was careless enough with a bow and arrow to shoot my own wife. But somethin' never seemed right about it. There was a man who caused me to miss my mark and another that wouldna let me near my dead wife. Ye and Euan were those men, I ken that now. Ye two killed Osla, didna ye?"

"What? Nay."

"Nay?" he asked. "Then mayhap ye need help rememberin' and I just need to choke the truth out of ye." He reached forward with his hands around the man's throat, but his friends rushed forward and pulled him off.

"Stop it, Hawke," said Ethan.

"The man is wounded and his hands bound," Orrick reminded him. "He can't defend himself."

"Leave him be, Hawke," said Caleb. "It's no' worth it."

"It is to me. I will no' be blamed for a feud between the clans any longer. I tell ye, I intend to prove ye did it and my name will finally be cleared after all this time. Someone get me my horse."

"Yer horse has been saddled for hours," said Logan, walking out of a stable with his horse ready to go.

"Where are ye goin'?" asked Hawke.

"We're comin' with ye." Ethan appeared from yet another stall.

"Nay, that wasna the plan."

"Well, we canna let ye get yerself killed without at least tryin' to save ye." Caleb grabbed the reins of his horse, too.

"Now wait a moment," said Hawke with a raised hand.

"I bathed and no longer stink so they willna smell me comin'," said Caleb with a smile.

"Who's goin' to guard the prisoner?"

"I'll stay here with Lennox," said Orrick, overhearing them and figuring out what they were going to do. "Please, be careful. I don't want to have to give the news to your father that you've perished."

"That's no' goin' to happen," said Hawke. "Let's go."

"Wait. What about Phoebe? Who's guardin' her?" asked Ethan.

"Blethers, that's right," said Hawke, running a weary hand through his tangled hair. He didn't want to have to post a guard at Phoebe's door. Not after the intimate time they'd spent together. Still, she had proven time and again that she couldn't be trusted. Mayhap he'd better not take the chance.

"Stableboy," he called to the boy watching the horses.

"Aye?" The boy rushed over.

"Keep guard at the first door above stairs in the tavern and do no' let the girl leave. Stay there until I return." He tossed the boy a coin.

"Aye, I will." The boy hurried out of the stable.

"Do no' ye mean *if* ye return?" asked Ethan.

"Ye're always a pessimist," complained Hawke.

"I saw a huge raven sitting atop the stable today. I think that means someone is goin' to die."

"Ye're also much too superstitious," said Hawke, pulling himself into the saddle. "Now let's go."

They rode through the dark toward Crookston Castle, but Hawke couldn't stop thinking about Phoebe. He also wondered if he should have brought Lennox along in case he got caught and needed the trade. Then again, this might be better. He had every hope of sneaking in and freeing his grandfather and getting out again before first light. And with his friends along now, he might just be able to do it.

"So, where's the postern gate?" asked Logan, as the castle came into view and they slowed their horses.

"I – I'm no' sure," said Hawke. "But it canna be that hard to find."

"Didna ye get the information out of Phoebe like ye planned?" asked Ethan.

"Nay."

"I thought ye said ye could do it," added Caleb.

"I . . . was distracted."

"God's eyes, ye bedded the girl," said Ethan with a laugh. "Well, she is comely and I canna say I blame ye."

"I never meant for it to go that far," admitted Hawke. "I only meant to get her relaxed so she'd spill her secrets."

"And instead ye spilled somethin' of yer own," said Logan.

"I hope ye're no' fallin' for the lass," said Caleb. "After all, she's the enemy and if this doesna work we'll have no choice but to trade her back to the MacNabs."

"We still have Lennox," Hawke reminded them. "And from what I've heard, he might be more valuable than the laird's daughter right now. Even though I'd like to kill the man instead of sendin' him back."

"Well, what's yer plan?" asked Ethan. "Walk right in through the front gate?"

"I dinna ken yet. Let me think."

"Well, think fast," said Logan. "The sun will be risin' soon."

* * *

PHOEBE AWOKE with a smile on her face, having made wonderful, exciting love with Hawke last night. She turned over in bed expecting to see him. But when the bed was empty, everything came back to her. It was his plan to seduce her to learn her secrets. She hadn't told him much, but still, he used her and left her.

"He's goin' to the castle," she said to herself, darting out of bed and getting herself together. She had to stop him. He'd be killed. She wasn't sure why she cared, but she did. Mayhap she could get back to the castle and sneak in through the postern gate before him. If she could manage to set the MacKeefes' laird free and heal her father, mayhap no one had to die.

She noticed her throwing knives sticking out from under a cloak and picked them up, putting one in her boot and strapping the other to her leg. If there was going to be any trouble, especially from Euan, she might need these.

Slowly opening the door, she peeked out. Hearing someone coming, she hurriedly snuck into the shadows and headed for the stable. Once there, she reached for a horse for quicker travel.

"Goin' somewhere, traitor?" came Lennox's voice from the dark. She'd almost forgotten he was there.

"Phoebe?" Orrick lit a lantern and walked out of the stall. "I thought Hawke put the stableboy at your door to guard it."

"So that's who I heard comin'," she said with a shake of her head.

"Where are you going?"

"Where did Hawke go?" she asked, instead of answering.

"They went to free their laird," said Lennox.

"They?" she asked. "Hawke's friends went with him?"

"Aye," said Orrick. "Phoebe, I hope you're not trying to escape."

She looked over at Lennox who was motioning for her to come closer.

"Nay, I'm here to see to Lennox's wound, that's all," she lied.

"I've already tended to it."

"I want Phoebe to check it. I dinna trust ye," snarled Lennox "Ye're the enemy and ye have been makin' it worse."

"Hush up," said Orrick, looking back at the door. "I don't want anyone to hear you."

"I'll get him to be quiet," said Phoebe. "Can I take a look at his wound?"

"All right, but be quick about it," said Orrick. "And whatever you do, don't untie him. Then you'd better get back to your room or Hawke will have my head when he returns."

"Of course," she assured him.

Walking over to Lennox, she figured she had to trust him. If there were two MacNabs working together, perhaps they could get back to the castle before any trouble broke out.

"Untie me," growled Lennox.

"No' yet." Phoebe looked back over her shoulder at Orrick. "Ye have to promise me that ye'll help me and stand against Euan. He's only tryin' to get rid of my faither, and I canna have that."

"Of course, I'll help ye, Phoebe. I never liked listenin' to Euan. He wants everythin' for himself and treats me like dirt."

"And if I untie ye, ye'll promise no' to hurt Hawke or any of his friends?"

"Look at me. I'm wounded and hurt and can barely move."

"All right," she finally agreed, hunkering down next to him. She took her throwing knife from under her skirt, noticing the way Lennox eyed her leg. She suddenly didn't trust him in the least. "Nay, I changed my mind," she said. But before she could move, Lennox grabbed her knife, pushing her down and hurriedly cutting the ropes that held his feet. "Give me that." She pushed up to her knees but he kicked at her next, sending her sprawling on the ground.

"What's going on?" asked Orrick, walking toward them from the door.

Lennox managed to cut the ropes at his wrists next. "Ye always were naught but a daft wench with straw in yer head," spat Lennox. "Euan and I should have killed ye long ago." Lennox started to come at her with the knife, but Orrick walked around the end of the stall.

"Nay! What are you doing?" asked the old man.

Instead of attacking her, Lennox turned, plunging the knife into Orrick's chest, and taking off at a run. He stole a horse and left the stable.

"Nay!" screamed Phoebe, crawling on her hands and knees to the old sorcerer. With tears in her eyes, she pulled her throwing knife from his chest. There was blood everywhere. "Orrick, I am so sorry," she cried, realizing his death would be her fault. "I didna mean for ye to die." Tears streamed down her cheeks.

"Hush, lassie, and get me my bag of herbs quickly and something to bind this wound." To her surprise, Orrick sat up without her help. He was a strong, determined man.

Phoebe rushed to the other end of the stall, grabbing Orrick's bag and hurrying back. "What can I do?" she asked, feeling so helpless. "This is all my fault. I am so sorry."

"First of all, calm down," said Orrick, not seeming at all panicked like she was.

"But ye're dyin', Orrick."

"Who said I'm dying?" He smiled and reached out for the bag.

"B-but Lennox stabbed ye in the heart." She cocked her head, surprised to see that there wasn't blood squirting out anymore.

"I'm a lot more resilient than you think, lassie. Now hush up and let me teach you a little more about healing herbs. Where is my book?"

"It's right here," she said, pulling it from her bag and wiping away another tear with the back of her hand.

"Let's wrap my wound and get back to your room where we can talk in private."

"My room? Ye want me to go back there?"

"Aye. Why? Were you planning on leaving? I don't think Hawke would like that. Plus, he's already going to be furious that we let Lennox escape."

"We didna let him escape, it just happened. No' to mention, Lennox stabbed ye. Och, Hawke is goin' to hate me now."

"Does it matter to you what he thinks? I thought you two were enemies."

"I'm no' so sure anymore, Orrick. But mayhap ye can look into yer crystal orb and tell me if Hawke thinks of me as an enemy or a lover."

"Nay, Phoebe. Only Hawke can tell you that. But I think if you look into your heart, you'll know the answer for yourself."

"Mayhap," she said, wanting to believe that Hawke thought she was more than an enemy. But she supposed a lot would depend on if Orrick died and how angry Hawke was going to be with her that Lennox escaped. Well, she'd find out when he and his friends returned. If they returned at all.

CHAPTER 17

Hawke snuck through the shadows of the courtyard, making his way to the dungeon of Crookston Castle. By sheer luck, he'd managed to find the secret entrance, and now he and his friends were on a mission to save his grandfather.

Logan and Ethan followed right behind him while Caleb stayed back with the horses, watching for trouble.

"There's the dungeon," whispered Hawke, looking up at the battlements to make sure the guards hadn't spotted them. There didn't seem to be a lot of the clan guarding the place, and he only hoped that most of them had gone to the coast to fight the English.

"Logan, stay here and cover our backs. Ethan, let's get in and out quickly. With any luck, they'll never know we were here until the mornin'."

Hawke hurried to the dungeon door, his sword at the ready. Then he and Ethan quietly slipped inside.

"How do ye ken he's in here?" whispered Ethan.

"I dinna ken for sure, but I thought it was a hell of a place to start lookin' for prisoners."

There was only one man guarding the door and Hawke

knocked him out with little trouble.

"Ye didna kill him?" asked Ethan in surprise, since Hawke had a reputation of killing first and asking questions later.

"I'm tryin' to quit," Hawke said under his breath, taking the keys from the guard and opening the gate leading to the cells. He picked up a torch and headed inside. "Stay here and watch my back," he told Ethan, in case anyone else entered the dungeon.

"Hurry," said Ethan. "The sun will be risin' soon."

Holding the torch high to guide his way, it didn't take him long to decipher that the cells were all empty except for one. He had thought it was the cell that held his grandfather but, to his surprise, two young women and a boy of about six years old occupied it instead.

"Who are ye?" asked the boy, looking up with big, hollow eyes. The three of them were gaunt and dirty. Hawke couldn't imagine why anyone would imprison women and children.

"Who are ye, is the real question," said Hawke. "And where are they keepin' the prisoner, Ian MacKeefe?"

"Ye're a MacKeefe," said the girl with long, blond hair.

"Why do ye say that?" he asked, scanning the surroundings. The place was a typical dungeon with cold stone and an occasional rat running by. But the stench in here of feces and urine told him that these prisoners hadn't even been given a pot to piss in. And by the looks of them, they'd barely been fed.

"Ye wear the same green and purple plaid of the prisoner," said the girl.

"Ye've seen my grandda?" asked Hawke, his spine stiffening. "Where are they keepin' him?"

"We dinna ken," said the other girl who looked a little older. She had curly brown hair and big round eyes. "We saw him when they brought him to the castle, but then they threw us in here and we havena seen anyone except for the auld man that brings us bread and water."

"Why are ye in here?"

"Euan took over the castle," cried the boy. "He doesna like us."

"But to imprison those of his own clan? And women and children, no less? Why?"

"Euan was waitin' until our faither dies, but he has already taken control of the castle now," said the first girl.

"He's goin' to ask ransom from the MacKeefes once they arrive and then he is goin' to kill our da and us as well," said the other girl.

"Please, help us," cried the boy. "I dinna want to die."

"Nay, I canna help ye, I'm sorry," said Hawke. "I am here only to bring back our laird." He turned to leave, not wanting to get involved. Two women and a boy were only going to slow him down and get him caught. He couldn't concern himself with what the MacNabs did, and neither did he need more MacNabs traveling with him. Two was already too many.

"I want Phoebe," whined the boy, crying aloud.

"Did ye say Phoebe?" Hawke stopped and turned around.

"She's our sister," said the blond. "Yer clan is holdin' her prisoner. She has been like a mathair to our brathair, Miles, since our mathair died in child birth."

"Then ye're Elspeth and Agan," he said.

"Aye," said the girls in surprise.

"I'm Elspeth," the darker-haired girl told him. "What is yer name?"

"I'm Hawke. Hawke MacKeefe," he said, swallowing the lump in his throat. How could he walk away from Phoebe's siblings after what they'd just told him? He rushed back to the cell and unlocked it.

"Ye're really goin' to help us?" asked Agan anxiously.

"I canna leave ye here under these conditions. Ye'll come with us."

"There are more of ye?"

"Aye, I am here with three of my friends."

"Hawke, I think someone's comin', and the sun is startin' to rise," said Ethan from the door. "I also had to hit the guard on the head again to keep him unconscious. Did ye find Ian?"

"Nay," said Hawke. "But we have three others who will be leavin' with us." He let out a deep breath, knowing that he wasn't going to be able to rescue his grandfather now. Instead, he had to see to the safety of the innocent women and the boy who just happened to be Phoebe's siblings. "Keep quiet and stay close," Hawke told them, leading the way, hoping he wouldn't regret this decision later on.

Hawke, Logan, and Ethan made it through the postern gate and to the horses just as the sun started to rise. Streams of bright light illuminated the castle, giving nowhere for them to hide.

"What's this and where's Ian?" asked Caleb as they exited the gate.

"That's what I said," grumbled Logan. "I'm no' here to save anyone but our laird."

"But these are Phoebe's siblings," said Hawke. "They were in the dungeon and I've yet to find Ian." He lifted the boy up onto Caleb's horse. "Caleb, take the boy. Logan and Ethan, take the girls."

"I hope ye're no' thinkin' about goin' back in there now," said Logan, helping Elspeth mount his horse and climbing up behind her.

"I canna leave without my grandfaither."

"He might be in the tower room with our faither," said Agan, letting Ethan help her to get atop his horse.

"What's the fastest way to get there unseen?" asked Hawke, looking back at the castle.

"It's impossible without bein' seen," said the girl.

"Give it up, Hawke," warned Caleb. "I see the guards lookin' over the battlements at us. Let's go."

"Intruders!" yelled one of the guards from atop the battlements. And before Hawke knew what was happening, they were being bombarded by arrows. Caleb's horse got spooked and reared up. Hawke saw the boy falling, and ran forward to keep him from hitting the ground. Caleb struggled with his horse to get it under control.

"I've got the boy, let's get the hell out of here," said Hawke, holding the boy while he mounted his horse quickly and led the way out of there. Thankfully, Hawke, his friends, and Phoebe's siblings weren't hit by an arrow. But as they rode away, Hawke looked back over his shoulder, wishing he could have saved his grandfather.

"I'll be back, Grandda," whispered Hawke. "I promise, I'll be back."

* * *

PHOEBE FLIPPED through the pages of Orrick's book, frantic to find something to help her know how to heal the sorcerer's chest wound. She swore the knife went through his heart. But if so, how could he have stood up and walked away with her? And why wasn't he bleeding profusely?

Her mind felt muddled and her legs shook.

"Calm down, Phoebe," said Orrick walking up behind her in the tavern chamber, resting his hand on her shoulder. When they came back to the room they found the stableboy standing guard. He felt foolish to be watching over an empty room. Orrick then dismissed him. Hawke was sure to be furious about what happened while he was gone.

"I ken there has to be somethin' to heal the heart," said Phoebe, scanning the pages quickly, not wanting Orrick to die. Too many people had already died needlessly and she felt it was her fault Orrick was injured. She should never have trusted Lennox. That was her downfall.

"Of course there is, but I don't need it." Orrick reached out and closed the book. Her eyes shot up to his.

"Aye, ye do. Ye were stabbed in the chest and –" Her gaze fell to the front of his tunic. "It's no longer bleedin'," she said, jumping up and inspecting the tunic, torn from the knife. "I dinna even see a wound," she said, gently touching him with her fingertips.

"I told you, I'm fine. Now stop worrying."

"But I saw ye get stabbed in the heart. Ye – ye should be dead!" She reached out and touched his chest again, checking for a wound.

"I'm a little different than most people," he told her, gently pushing her hand away.

"What are ye?" she asked, backing away from him. "Are ye some sort of a – a devil or a demon or a – warlock?"

"I'm a sorcerer," he said with a laugh. "I'm not a devil or demon or even a warlock. I'm just . . . different."

"How is it ye can get stabbed with a knife and no' even bleed? Show me yer wound."

The sorcerer smiled and shook his head. "My story is a fascinating, yet a sad one I'm afraid."

"What does that mean? Tell me more."

"Nay, I can't tell you my story. Not now. It's not important, Phoebe. What is important is your relationship with Hawke."

"What do ye mean?" Shyly, she looked the other way, wondering if he knew they'd made love. "Did ye see somethin' in yer gazin' orb havin' to do with us?"

"I didn't need to. These walls are thin and your shutter wasn't closed all the way over the window last night, so the sound traveled down to the stable."

"Och, I'm embarrassed," she said, holding a hand over her face. "I never meant for it to happen. But once it did – neither of us could stop."

"It's a normal thing to couple. An attraction between two people can sometimes lead to intimacy."

"Have ye ever been intimate with a lady?" she asked, wondering if Orrick was ever married or if he had children.

"I told you . . . my story is not important, Phoebe. Concentrate instead on what you're going to do and what you can learn about healing."

There was commotion outside and the sound of running horses. Then they suddenly came to a stop. Phoebe hurried to the window and peered out. Relief washed through her when she saw Hawke and his friends riding up to the tavern. "It's Hawke," she cried.

"Is Ian with them?" asked Orrick, hurrying over to the window as well.

"That's odd. Three of them are ridin' double," she said, leaning out the window to see more clearly in the rising sun. When she realized who they brought back with them, she gasped.

"What is it, Phoebe?" asked Orrick.

"They've brought my sisters and brathair with them. Why would they do that?"

"I don't see Ian anywhere." Orrick scowled as he scanned the grounds. "Something is wrong."

"I need to find out why my siblin's are here." Phoebe ran across the room and threw open the door, heading down the stairs to the main area that was the tavern. They had no customers this early in the morning. Leaving the building, she ran out to greet them.

"Agan, Elspeth, Miles, what are ye doin' here?" she asked.

Logan was helping Elspeth from the horse. The girl looked up and smiled. "Phoebe, ye're all right."

"We were so worried about ye," said Agan as both of the girls ran over to hug her.

"Phoebe," called out her little brother. She turned to see Hawke carrying Miles to her. He looked good with a child in his arms.

"Go to yer sister," he said, putting the boy on the ground. Miles ran over and hugged her as well.

"What happened to ye all?" asked Phoebe, shocked by the state and condition of her siblings. "Ye are all dirty and smelly and look as if ye havena eaten in weeks."

"He put us in the dungeon and threatened to kill us," said Miles, brushing a tear from his eye.

"Who did?" asked Phoebe.

"It was Euan," Elspeth told her. "He's taken over the castle."

"What about faither? Is he – is he . . ." She couldn't bring herself to say the word.

"He's alive, but barely," Agan told her. "Phoebe, if he doesna die of his own illness, Euan is goin' to kill him."

"PHOEBE, why are ye out here instead of in yer room?" asked Hawke, noticing the stableboy in the shadows and Orrick standing next to her. "And who is watchin' Lennox?"

"Oh, that." Phoebe's smile faded fast. Hawke's heart went out to her. He loved seeing her reunion with her siblings. But he had to remember that she was still his prisoner. Even if she was his lover now as well.

"Lennox escaped," Orrick broke in, coming to Phoebe's defense.

"Blethers!" spat Hawke. "He was tied up hand and foot. How did that happen?"

"He – he knocked me down and stole a horse," said Orrick, rubbing his chest.

"It's all right, Orrick," Phoebe told the sorcerer, gently laying her hand on his arm. Then she looked up at Hawke, raised her chin, and answered.

"I cut him loose with my throwing knife that I found in our room."

"Yer room? As in both of ye?" asked Agan with wide eyes.

"Never mind that," grumbled Hawke. "Phoebe, were ye tryin' to escape again?"

"Aye, I did consider it," she bravely admitted. "I heard ye

talkin' with yer friends about goin' to Crookston Castle and sneakin' in and rescuin' yer grandda. I wanted to go home, Hawke. Ye canna blame me. I shouldna be a prisoner." She reached out and picked up her brother while her sisters moved closer and put their arms around her shoulders. "I dinna belong here. I need to get home to my faither before it is too late."

"I ken," he said softly, feeling as if he did the wrong thing by keeping her as his prisoner. He was more than the enemy now. They'd made love and it was welcomed by both of them. He thought of her as his friend, his lassie. His lover. She had asked if he felt that way but he wasn't able to admit it. One of the reasons he'd tried to rescue his grandfather without trading Phoebe was because, in his heart, he honestly didn't want her to leave him. But now, seeing how close she was with her siblings, he started to think that she did need to go back to her father. The man needed her. She needed him. But with Euan in charge and now with Lennox gone and probably back at the man's side, he was sure Crookston Castle wasn't a safe place for Phoebe or her siblings to be. "My grandda doesna deserve to be a prisoner either."

"Where is yer grandda?" asked Phoebe, her brows dipping as she spoke.

"I wasna able to rescue him."

"Why no'?" she asked.

"Because he was too busy savin' yer siblin's," said Caleb. "I still do no' understand why we risked our lives to gain more prisoners and still havena rescued our chieftain."

"I wanted to go back to get him, but the MacNabs started to attack," Hawke told Phoebe. "I needed to protect yer siblin's, so I decided to bring them back here right away."

"Ye did that? For me?" Her hazel eyes locked with his, showing gratitude and respect. "Thank ye, Hawke. "Thank ye, from the bottom of my heart. Now all we need to do is to rescue my faither."

"We?" Hawked raised a brow. "Ye are no' goin' anywhere near

Crookston Castle, lassie. As a matter of fact, we're goin' to head to the Highlands right away."

"We are?" asked Phoebe. "Ye're takin' my siblin's there as well?"

"We are?" echoed Logan in surprise.

"Ye heard me. Pack up, everyone," instructed Hawke. "Orrick, get the wagon. The children will ride with ye."

"Hawke, what are ye thinkin'?" Ethan and Logan approached him.

"We canna take all these MacNabs to the MacKeefe camp," protested Logan.

"Well, what do ye suggest we do?" asked Hawke. "They canna go back to Crookston Castle. Ye saw how Euan had them imprisoned. They are no' safe there."

"Leave them here," suggested Caleb.

"At a tavern?" Hawke raised a brow. "The Horn and Hoof is hardly a place for women and children. Plus, I dinna want to endanger Callum. His tavern has always been a neutral ground where Highlanders and Lowlanders and sometimes even the English could meet without confrontation. I willna jeopardize that for him. Just bringin' our prisoners here to begin with was risky and no' a smart thing to do. If the MacNabs come lookin' for trouble, they're goin' to find it."

"Ye're right," said Logan with a nod. "We'll head to the Highlands right away."

"Phoebe, I'm scared," whimpered Miles, clinging to her skirt.

"It'll all right, Brathair, dinna worry." Phoebe rubbed her hand up and down the boy's back. "Hawke will protect us."

As Phoebe and her siblings headed for the stable, she hoped it was true. Because if Euan and his men came looking for them, there wasn't much she could do to protect her siblings by herself. She was counting on Hawke and his clan now to keep them all safe. Ironic, since the only man who could protect her and her siblings was also her captor.

CHAPTER 18

"I still dinna understand why we didna go back to save Ian," complained Caleb as the small entourage made their way to the MacKeefe camp. Ethan rode alongside of them with his wolfhound and Logan brought up the rear with his wolf slinking along in the shadows. Apollo glided above them doing lazy circles in the sky.

Phoebe and her siblings were behind them in the cart. She wanted to stay with her sisters and brother, so Hawke let her do that instead of making her ride with him. He didn't think she'd try to escape and leave her siblings here. He also felt like he needed to be away from her to be able to clear his head. Ever since they'd made love, things were different.

"We canna do that right now," said Hawke, looking straight ahead as they rode. "I have to protect Phoebe and the boy, and her sisters."

"Since when do we put protectin' the enemy in front of savin' one of our own clan?" rallied Logan.

"Ever since he slept with the lass," said Caleb, releasing a puff of air from his mouth.

"Hawke, think what ye're doin'," said Logan.

"I am," he answered.

"But ye're makin' a stupid decision."

"Am I?" Hawke asked. "After all, dinna forget we promised my faither we'd get to the MacKeefe camp to protect our own lassies and bairns so that is where we'll go."

"The English willna come this far," Caleb assured him. "I talked to a few men at the tavern that told me there was some suspicion that Richard was goin' to turn his troops around and head back to England. The Scots are holdin' out as long as they can."

"I dinna ken," said Logan. "They also told us that the English were still headin' north up the coast."

"No matter what happens with the English, we have women and children to protect and Phoebe and her siblin's are no exception," stated Hawke.

"What's the plan for savin' our chieftain?" asked Caleb. "Are we goin' to trade all of them for him?"

"I dinna ken," said Hawke, feeling broken-hearted already. He didn't want Phoebe or her sisters and brother to go back to Crookston Castle while Euan ruled. "Her faither is ill and might be dyin'."

"So might yer grandda, or did ye forget about him?"

"I didna forget," snapped Hawke. "Now both of ye leave me alone. I need to think." Hawke urged his horse into a full gallop, distancing himself from the others. Perhaps when he arrived home, he'd head up into the mountains to clear his mind and come up with a plan. So much and so many depended on him. If only he hadn't fallen for Phoebe and seen her siblings locked away in the dungeon, then perhaps things would be different right now.

* * *

Phoebe rode next to Orrick on the bench of the wagon on their way to the MacKeefe camp. She noticed Hawke kept to himself, not even conversing much with his friends.

"What's troubling you, Phoebe?" asked Orrick. Phoebe glanced over her shoulder into the back of the wagon. Her sisters and brother were sleeping. Hawke had made sure to give them food and ale, and they felt safe for the first time since they'd been locked in the dungeon by Euan.

"I was just thinkin' about my faither," she told him. "He is ill and I'm afraid he will die before I return to Crookston Castle."

"Have you tried to heal him with the herbs you read about in my book?"

"Aye," she said. "Most of them. However, I wish I had some of that Common Centaury. I am sure that could heal him. It has to."

"Phoebe, there is something I didn't mention about that plant that I think you need to know."

"I ken. It only grows on the Isle of Kerrera."

"Besides that. You see, it is biennial."

"Biennial?" she asked.

"Aye. That means it only blooms once every two years."

"And ye said it is bloomin' right now?"

"That's right. If you can't collect some of it soon, you'll have to wait two more years to gather it."

"Nay!" she exclaimed. "I canna wait that long. My faither will die by then."

"Then you'll have to figure out a way to get to the island," he told her. "It's the only way. But you'll have to do it soon, because the blooming season doesn't last long for Common Centaury or Hart's Tongue. Ye'll need them both to cure yer faither."

"I will find a way," she told him, determined to help heal her father at any cost. "I will find a way to gather the plants and bring them back to Crookston Castle to heal my faither."

"Even if you do find a way, Phoebe, I'm not sure you'll be able to go back to the castle. You heard what Hawke said earlier. I have a feeling he is not going to let you out of his sight."

Phoebe released a sigh and looked back once more at her siblings. She wanted to save her father but, at the same time, she'd always been like a mother to Elspeth, Agan and Miles. She didn't want to let any of them down. She couldn't do this alone. If she was going to accomplish these things, she was going to need help. Hawke's help. And right now, she had the feeling he wasn't going to be in a very generous mood.

A little while later, Hawke led the way into the MacKeefe camp, greeted happily by a dozen children who ran to meet him. They shouted excitedly and jumped up and down, all gathering around him.

"What did ye bring us, Hawke?" asked one little boy.

"I want a ride on yer horse," said another.

"Hawke, we missed ye," said one of the younger girls. "We're so happy ye're back."

"Now, calm down, all of ye," he said with a chuckle, dismounting and slipping his hand into his pouch. "I have somethin' in my hand. Whoever can guess what it is can have it."

"It's a sweetmeat," said one of the girls.

"Nay, it's a flower," said a teenage girl with red hair, blushing and looking to the ground.

"Och, dinna be silly," said one of the boys. "He brought us a weapon."

"A weapon?" Hawke laughed and held out his closed fist. "What weapon could fit in my closed hand, Finlay?"

"I ken, I ken. It's a coin," said a little boy with dark curly hair and rosy cheeks that was only about the age of Miles.

"Nay, Liam, it's no' that." He bent down and held out his fist to the boy. "Think hard. What could I possibly fit in my hand?"

"I dinna ken," said the little boy.

"It's small," Hawke told him. "It's somethin' from nature that sometimes gets stuck in yer shoe."

"A rock?" asked the boy.

"Aye, lad. Ye got it. And this rock is very special." He opened up his hand to show the children an oblong, smooth rock that looked like an egg.

"A rock?" asked Finlay, sounding disappointed. "What's so special about a rock?"

"This isna just any rock. Gather around," said Hawke, causing the children to move in closer. "The fairies of the hills say that this rock was once the egg of a powerful dragon."

"A dragon?" Miles got out of the cart and ran over to join the children. Agan and Elspeth followed.

"The legend says that at night on the first full moon of the month, the rock turns back into a dragon's egg. And if ye take guid care of it, it might even hatch."

"Hatch?" asked Liam with wide eyes. "So I might have my very own dragon?"

"I want one," cried Finlay.

"Me, too," shouted another of the children.

"I'll tell ye what," said Hawke. "For now, Liam can carry it around, and tomorrow it will go to . . ." Hawke looked from face to face and all the children waited with bated breath. They all seemed so excited as they pushed forward eagerly. Miles and Phoebe's sisters stood at the back of the group. No one talked to them "Tomorrow it goes to . . . Miles," he said.

Miles' head snapped up and he wet his lips with his tongue.

"Who?" asked one of the children.

"My new friend, Miles," said Hawke. "And after that, he will pass it on to another child and that will continue every day."

"Who are they?" asked one of the little girls, pointing at Phoebe's sisters.

"These are some of my friends. Miles, and his sisters, Elspeth and Agan. And Phoebe," he said, extending an open arm toward Phoebe as she climbed out of the wagon.

"They dinna belong to our clan. Look at their red plaids," said Finlay.

"That's right," said Hawke.

"Which clan are they?" asked a little girl.

"We're the MacNabs," said Miles before Hawke could stop him.

"The MacNabs are our enemies! My da told me so." Finlay crossed his arms over his chest.

"Well, mayhap some of them are, but I assure ye that these four are our friends," Hawke told the children. "Now, mayhap some of ye can show them around the camp?"

"I will, I will," cried a little girl holding her hand in the air.

"Go as a group," said Hawke, sending them on their way.

"Hawke!" A woman with dark hair streaked with gray at the temples ran out from one of the huts made of wattle and daub. She threw her arms around him.

"Hello, Mathair," said Hawke, taking the woman into his arms and giving her a big hug and a kiss atop her head. It melted Phoebe's heart to see how the children flocked to Hawke. She also enjoyed seeing him with his mother. He had a much softer, vulnerable side to him that she hadn't witnessed before now.

"Orrick, so glad to see you, too. I didn't expect you. But who is this, Hawke?" The woman looked straight at Phoebe. She spoke like an Englishwoman, but dressed like a Scot.

"This is Phoebe MacNab, Mathair," Hawke told her. "Phoebe, this is my mathair, Wren."

"You're a MacNab?" Wren released Hawke, seeming confused. "Hawke, the pigeon your father sent from Hermitage Castle said the MacNabs captured Ian."

"Aye. And I captured Phoebe."

Wren glanced over to Phoebe's siblings. "You . . . seem to have more than just one prisoner."

"Those are Phoebe's siblin's, Mathair. Is that haggis I smell?" asked Hawke, sniffing the air.

"It is," said Wren, flashing a smile. "You and your father like it so much, I am sure to always have some at the ready. Come, and we'll have something to eat."

"Phoebe will join us," said Hawke, reaching out and taking her by the arm.

"Of course." Wren's eyes darted to her son and then back. Phoebe had the feeling Hawke's mother somehow knew they'd made love. It was almost as if she could see right through her.

"Tend to the horses first, Hawke, and then meet us by the fire," said Wren.

"Caleb and the others will get the horses," Hawke told her.

"Go," said Wren, giving her son a slight push. "This will give Phoebe and me a little time to get to know each other."

"That's what I'm afraid of," mumbled Hawke, heading back to the stable.

"What did ye mean about the pigeons?" asked Phoebe as she headed toward the main fire with Wren.

"That is something my brother, Madoc, set up," Wren explained. "He raises carrier pigeons. He used to race them but now they carry messages back and forth from Hermitage Castle to the Highlands, and even to Blake Castle in Devonshire where my other brother, Corbett lives. It's very useful to get information in a hurry."

"I suppose so."

"How is Hawke treating you?" Wren glanced over from the corners of her eyes.

"What do ye mean?" Could she possibly know they'd been intimate together?

"You're a prisoner, but also a woman. I wanted to make sure he was treating you with respect."

"Och, aye, he is."

"And do you like him?" She stopped and turned toward Phoebe.

"He's my captor," she reminded Wren.

"I assume you mean a lot to him. After all, he entered this camp with you and your siblings, rather than returning here with my father-in-law."

"He tried to save Ian, but he found my siblin's in the dungeon in my own castle. Euan is a wretch and has taken over."

"Is your father still alive?"

"Aye, but barely. If I dinna find the proper plants and herbs to heal him, he will die soon."

"And Hawke knows this?"

She nodded.

"I see," she answered in thought. "Did you know Osla MacNab?"

"Aye. She was my cousin. We were close and like sisters."

"Hawke was married to her for a short while in an attempt to align with your clan."

"I ken." Her teeth clenched. "He killed her and continued this feud between our clans."

"You can't really believe that, can you?"

"Well, mayhap no'," she said, looking to the ground, thinking about her special time with Hawke, as well as the way he loved children and saved her siblings. "How did it happen?"

"That is a conversation you should have with him. But I will tell you that it wasn't his fault that she died, however, he blames himself. To this day, he tries to protect all women and children trying to make up for what happened."

"All right, the horses are tended to, now can we eat?" asked Hawke, walking up to join them.

"Hawke?" His mother looked at him knowingly and smiled. "You couldn't have finished that so fast."

"Och, all right, Mathair, I didna. But Caleb and the others dinna need me to do it. I am hungry and really wanted some food."

"Really?" asked Wren. "I think I know you better than that,

Son. You were wondering what we were talking about and it was driving you mad so you had to join us."

"Me?" Hawke hit his palm against his chest. "I dinna ken what ye mean, Mathair."

His hawk screeched from above them and Hawke held out his arm as a perch. The bird glided down, frightening Phoebe with its size as it gently landed on Hawke's arm with a dead vole in its mouth.

"Och," she cried, holding her hand over her head.

"He's no' goin' to hurt ye, lassie," said Hawke with a chuckle.

"But it's so big!"

Hawke waggled his brows. "Some of the lassies say the same thing about me."

"They do? How many lassies?" Phoebe lowered her arm and stared at Hawke, feeling a little jealous.

"Hawke, there will be no more talk like that around here with so many children listening," scolded his mother.

"Sorry, Mathair. Go," he told his bird, sending it from his arm. "Ye got me in trouble with more than one lass," he mumbled under his breath. The hawk took off up into a tree to eat the rodent.

"During our meal, I want to hear all about it," said Wren.

"Mathair!" Hawke made a face. "And ye say I need to watch what I say around the children?"

"Hawke, I was talking about the attacks by the MacNabs and your attempt to rescue Ian. However, I have a feeling you two are thinking about something else." She smiled at the both of them.

"I think they might need my help in the stable after all," said Hawke, taking a few steps backward and taking off at a brisk pace.

Phoebe looked at Wren and smiled. "Hawke isna really that bad of a captor after all."

"That's what I thought," she told Phoebe. "Just do me a favor, Phoebe and don't break my son's heart. He has gone through some tough times and I never thought he'd ever fall in love with a woman after Osla died."

"In love?" she asked, her heart skipping a beat. "Och, I'm sure Hawke doesna love me."

"I've seen the way you two look at each other and it's no secret. Just like Hawke's father and me, once again, enemies have turned into lovers."

CHAPTER 19

Hawke sat at the trestle table in the main longhouse as they ate. This is where most of the MacKeefes gathered to share meals. There were many smaller huts for the different families to live in and also an infirmary. Half the infirmary was used for the ailing and the other half as a place for guests and visitors to sleep.

Over the years, the Highland camp grew larger and larger. Hawke's sisters and their families, as well as Caleb, Logan, and Ethan's siblings and families all lived here or at Hermitage Castle.

The camp lay in the mountains just outside of Oban. It connected with Loch Linnhe, one of the only lochs that opened to the sea. The hills were dotted with the MacKeefes' longhorn cattle as well as the Highland sheep. It was beautiful in the Highlands and Hawke preferred to stay here instead of at the castle in the Lowlands.

Phoebe sat quietly next to Hawke as they ate. Her sisters and brother were across from her, eagerly devouring the meal.

"I was sure we were goin' to die in the dungeon," said Elspeth. "Phoebe, we thought ye were goin' to die with the MacKeefes, but now I see it isna so."

"I like it better here than at Crookston Castle," said the boy, Miles. He sat next to Liam and some of the other children he'd befriended since he arrived. Liam was Hawke's sister, Heather's boy while Finlay was his sister Lark's child.

"When are ye goin' to bring back our laird?" asked one of the men of the clan. "It seems that should have been a priority over savin' the prisoners!"

"I agree," grumbled someone else, making Hawke feel very uncomfortable.

"My son did what he felt was right," Wren told them. "You all need to give him some time."

"But Ian might be dead by then!"

"We need to save him now," called out someone else.

"Please," said Wren. "Our defenses are low since some of our men went to fight the English and others are protecting Hermitage Castle. We can't save Ian right now."

"Nay, they're right," said Hawke, throwing down his spoon and getting to his feet. "I never should have left the enemy's castle without our laird. I'm goin' back to get him in the mornin'."

"Then I'm goin' with ye," said Logan, also standing.

"Count me in," said Ethan, getting up from the table.

"Ye're no' leavin' without me," add Caleb, grabbing a piece of bread and getting to his feet.

"Hawke," said Phoebe, from beside him. "Take me, too."

"Nay," protested Phoebe's sister, Agan. "Phoebe, ye dinna want to go back there. Euan will probably kill ye."

"I need to go," she said bravely. "I have to help heal faither. Besides, they can use me for a trade."

"Nay, ye're no' goin'," snapped Hawke, turning and walking to the door. "I'll go alone at first light. No one else will be put in danger or killed because of my mistake."

* * *

PHOEBE RAN AFTER HAWKE, heading him off as he left the building.

"Hawke, ye canna do this alone."

"Get out of my way, Phoebe." He stepped around her and headed for the loch. Phoebe ran after him.

"Hawke, stop! I need to talk to ye."

"There is nothin' to say," he answered and continued walking. "I've made my decision."

"But ye'll be killed."

"Then so be it," he said. "If I die, I'll be doin' it for a worthy cause."

"I love ye," she blurted out before she could stop herself from saying it.

He stopped in his tracks and turned around. "What did ye say?"

"Ye heard me. I've fallen in love with ye and I think ye've fallen in love with me, too."

"Nay. We're enemies."

"So was Osla, but yet ye were married to her. Did ye love her?"

Hawke looked up to the sky where his hawk was making lazy circles above them. Then he let out a sigh and held out his hand to her.

"Come with me, Phoebe."

"Where are we goin'?" she asked, reaching out and taking his hand.

"I think we need to talk in private and I have just the place to do it."

"All right," she said, curious as to where he was taking her.

They walked down the hill and to the shore where she saw a small fishing boat tied up at the dock.

"It's a boat," she said excitedly.

"Aye. It's my boat. I use it sometimes to sail out to the ocean to think and be alone."

"It looks big enough to fare the sea."

"Aye, it is. I let the clan use it to fish. It's small enough to maneuver easily with just one person."

"Really," she said as he helped her board. "Can we go for a ride?"

"I suppose so." Hawk set the sails and expertly manned the boat while she watched, taking in every little thing he did.

"This is wonderful," she said, as they headed out to sea. With the wind in her hair and the light spray of salt water against her face, she closed her eyes and leaned back on the seat, taking in the feel of the warm sun.

"I didna have time to fall in love with her," said Hawke, causing Phoebe to open her eyes.

"What?" she asked, sitting up to look at him.

"Osla," he said, staring out to sea, manning the rudder as the boat pushed through the water. "I was young when we were married to make an alliance between our clans."

"I remember," she said. "Even though I was only a child at the time. My clan thinks ye killed her. That is why the feud continues."

"I didna kill her," he said, a dark shadow washing over his face.

"That's what yer mathair said. Tell me, how did it happen?" asked Phoebe, scooting closer to him.

"I am no' exactly sure. We were on a huntin' trip. I separated from Osla when I thought I heard a deer in the woods. I was usin' a bow and arrows. I missed the deer and my arrow went astray. And when I returned, one of my arrows was stickin' out of her back. One of the MacNabs pulled it out and tested for signs of life, but she was already dead. I was one MacKeefe huntin' with the MacNab Clan at the time. Of course, when they saw what happened, I was blamed and the feud continued."

"Oh, that's awful." Phoebe held her stomach, not wanting to think of her cousin dying such a horrible death.

"It was my fault in a way."

"I thought ye just said it wasna."

"I didna kill her, but I failed to protect her. So, I am to blame for Osla's death after all."

"Nay, that's no' true. It sounds to me as if ye were set up. By one of the MacNabs, no doubt. Were Euan and Lennox along on the hunt, too?"

"I didna ken them at the time, but I do now. Aye, they were there, and Euan was the one who wouldna let me near my dead wife."

"I'm sure they must have killed her."

"I have my suspicions that it might be true. But how am I supposed to prove Osla didna die by one of my stray arrows?"

"I dinna ken, Hawke. I am sorry." Phoebe noticed islands far out on the water. "Is one of those the Isle of Kerrera?"

"Aye," he answered. "The one in the middle. But dinna even think about goin' there."

"Why no'?" she asked. "It is the only place to get the Common Centaury and Hart's Tongue that I need to heal my faither."

"The island is haunted. No one goes there unless they want to be cursed." He started to turn the boat around.

"I didna think ye'd be afraid of a superstition."

He looked at her and his eyes settled on her lips. "I'm no'. And to address what ye said earlier, Phoebe, I've never had anyone say they loved me before."

"Really?" She moved closer and reached over and kissed him on the mouth. "I dinna ken why no'. After all, ye are attractive, a mighty warrior, and . . . guid at makin' love." Just thinking of when they made love had Phoebe's mind going in several different directions. She couldn't stop thinking about how she'd cried out in elation, not once, but twice that night.

"Just . . . guid? That's it?" he asked playfully, sitting next to her and pulling her into his arms.

"I suppose . . . great would be what I meant to say," she answered with a giggle.

"Ye hesitated." He reached out and trailed his hand down her cheek. "That tells me ye werena sure." His fingers moved lower, brushing against her collarbone and grazing over her breast. Then with one fingertip, he encircled one of her nipples, right through her clothes. Phoebe inhaled, feeling a delicious shiver run through her.

"I suppose . . . practice makes perfect?" she teased him, putting her hand on his bare leg and pushing up under his plaid and between his thighs. When her hand touched his erection, she almost jumped, realizing he wore no braies. "Hawke, dinna ye wear braies under yer plaid?"

"No' always. Does it excite ye?"

She wrapped her hand around his hardened form and squeezed lightly. Now it was his turn to gasp. His body stiffened and he closed his eyes partially.

"Och, aye, it excites me," she told him, pushing up his plaid to gaze upon his aroused form. Then, throwing caution to the wind, she did something she'd heard the other women of the clan talking about that men supposedly loved. She never thought she'd try this, but something made her do it. She bent down and placed her mouth on him.

"Bid the devil!" he cried out, pushing his knees apart, holding on to her head. "Phoebe, if ye keep that up, I'll be finished before ye begin."

"Dinna ye like it?" She looked up and smiled.

"Too much," he told her, pulling her up to a standing position, slipping his hands under her skirt and pulling down her braies. She stepped out of them, holding on to his shoulders. He pushed up her gown and pulled it off over her head.

"Hawke! I'm naked. Someone might see us. Did ye forget we're on a boat in the middle of the water?"

"Nay, I didna forget. And dinna worry, there is no one around.

Do ye want to make love on the water, Phoebe? Would that excite ye?"

"Aye, I do," she admitted, feeling herself already climbing as her excitement grew.

He reached up and cupped one of her bare breasts in his large palm, holding her around the waist as he sat, helping her to maintain balance. Then his lips closed over her nipple, suckling, pulling, teasing. Her knees went weak beneath her, and she felt as if she were losing balance with the sway of the boat on the water.

"Sit on my lap, Phoebe."

"Like last time? When we made love standing and up against the wall?" she asked. When she started to sit facing him, he stopped her.

"Nay, no' like that. Like this." He turned her around, his hands on her hips.

"Hawke, I dinna understand. How can we –"

He spread her legs and pulled her down on his lap, her back to his chest. Leaning her forward, he fondled her breasts as he slipped his shaft into her warmth.

"Och!" she said, feeling excited. A pulse deepened between her thighs.

"Ride me," he told her. "Like ye are ridin' astride."

Their bodies glided together, apart and back together with liquid passion guiding them in their lovemaking. Phoebe's back arched and she held on to his knees, feeling naughty but yet excited to be doing something like this in the open and on a boat no less! And when she climbed to her peak, she threw back her head and cried out, not caring if anyone could or would hear her. All that mattered was that moment. The only thing that was important was making love with Hawke. He was gentle, taking his time, making sure she was sated before he cried out her name on the wind.

It was magical and special. And when they'd both been sated, she straddled him the other way and they held their bodies together as they continued to kiss.

"I never even had time to remove my plaid," he told her.

"Ye didna even need to," she said. "Hawke, let's go for a swim. It's such a beautiful day."

"I'd like that," he said, kissing her on the nose. "Let me drop the anchor and we'll take a dip." He dropped the anchor as well as his plaid and then reached out and scooped her up into his arms, trying his best to keep his balance as the waves rocked them back and forth.

She giggled, liking this playful side of Hawke.

"Ye'd better be careful, Phoebe. Ye dinna want to fall overboard." He climbed up on the bench with her still in his arms.

"Hawke, put me down," she said, laughing all the while. "We're goin' to fall."

"Nay, we're no' goin' to – oops," he said, falling into the water with her still in his arms. They played and kissed in the water, and finally as the sun started to set, they climbed aboard.

"Here," he said, handing her his plaid to use to dry off before getting dressed. "We'd better get back. It's gettin' dark, and I'll need to prepare for tomorrow."

"Aye," she said, wiping off her face as he raised the anchor. "Hawke, I dinna want anythin' to happen to ye tomorrow. It's too dangerous. Please dinna go."

"I've made my decision," he told her. "Sometimes, there are things we just have to do and no one at all is goin' to stop us."

"I see," she said, drying her face in his plaid, looking over her shoulder at the isles in the distance. Yes, she thought. Sometimes there were things a person needed to do, and no one was going to stop them.

CHAPTER 20

As soon as night set in and everyone was asleep, Phoebe got out of bed and tiptoed over to where Orrick was sleeping. Her sisters and brother were on pallets spread across the floor, sleeping peacefully.

"Orrick," she whispered putting a gentle hand on the man's shoulder. Lying on his back, he opened one sleepy eye and then the other.

"What is it, Phoebe?" he whispered back.

They slept in the infirmary, where the guests were housed. Thankfully, Hawke and his friends had huts of their own where they stayed. Not wanting to leave the prisoners unguarded, Ethan's wolfhound stayed watch with Orrick. The men tried to leave Jack, Logan's wolf there as well, but the animal needed to roam free. Plus, Phoebe's little brother, Miles, was afraid of it. Of course, Hawke didn't think Phoebe would try to escape with her siblings there now, and she wouldn't. If it wasn't for her father still being at the castle, she wouldn't even want to go there again.

"I need yer help. Grab yer bag of herbs and follow me." With her bag slung over her shoulder, Phoebe tiptoed past the sleeping hound, only managing to get to the door before the dog was up and standing in front of her.

"Hello, Trapper," she said, running a hand over its head. "Let me pass, please." When she took a step, the dog growled.

"Now, now, there," said Orrick, holding out a bone to the dog. The dog took it eagerly and lay down to chew on it, letting them pass.

"Where did ye get a bone?" asked Phoebe, impressed, as they left the infirmary.

"I'm a sorcerer, Phoebe. I saved it from dinner, seeing that I would need it tonight."

"Ye ken that I'd be askin' for yer help?" she asked in surprise.

"Aye. And I have a feeling I know where we're going, but I warn you, Hawke isn't going to like this."

"Hawke will never find out. We'll be to the isle and back before he even awakes. Now, I only hope ye ken how to sail a boat."

They made it to the boat quickly in the dark. Phoebe kept looking back over her shoulder but, thankfully, no one followed. They traveled only by the light of the moon.

"I'd think you'd try to escape and go back to Crookston Castle instead," said Orrick.

"Nay. I willna leave my siblin's here without me. And I willna go back to the castle without the means to heal my faither. Will we be able to find the Common Centaury and Hart's Tongue in the dark?"

"Aye. I know exactly where to find it, and also how to get to the island since I've been there before."

"Great," said Phoebe excitedly. "Here's the boat."

They boarded the boat and were about to push off when Phoebe heard a noise from inside the cabin. She looked over to see Hawke bent over, staring out the small door. "Goin' somewhere, lass?"

"Hawke!" Phoebe stiffened. She'd been caught and now he'd keep her from her mission.

The sound of a barking dog drew her attention in the opposite direction. Her head whipped around to see Trapper bounding down to the lake with Ethan running right behind him.

"She's gettin' away," cried Ethan, running with his dog onto the pier. "Trapper came to get me."

"Aye, a little late for that," said Hawke, stepping out and straightening up to his full height. "Orrick, I'm surprised that ye'd be a part of all this deceit," Hawke told the sorcerer.

"I'm sorry, Hawke. It's just that she asked for my help and I couldn't turn her down because it is for a good purpose. Besides, I have an interest in this, too. It's only once every two years that the Common Centaury blooms. I'm in desperate need of it myself."

"Phoebe," said Hawke, looking down at her in the moonlight. A bluish glow encompassed him.

"I ken what ye're goin' to say." Phoebe hung her head and wished that she hadn't been caught. "I'll head back to camp at once."

"If ye do that, how are ye ever goin' to collect that silly plant?" asked Hawke.

Phoebe's head snapped up. "What did ye say?"

"Come on, let's raise the sails and get to the isle and back before daybreak. I have our laird to save come mornin'."

"Thank ye, Hawke!" Phoebe threw her arms around Hawke's shoulders, giving him a hug and a kiss. The action rocked the boat and Orrick fell onto the seat.

"Hold on, I think I'd better come with ye," said Ethan, jumping into the boat, being followed by his hound. "If anyone is goin' on a journey in the middle of the night, I will no' be left out."

"I am so excited," said Phoebe as they set sail.

"So, where is it exactly that we are goin'?" asked Ethan,

helping Hawke man the lines. His dog put its front paws up on the side of the boat and eagerly looked over the edge, panting.

"We're goin' to the Isle of Kerrera to collect some Common Centaury and Hart's Tongue to heal my faither," said Phoebe excitedly.

"The Isle of Kerrera?" Ethan frowned and shook his head. "Nay, that isle's said to have a haunted castle and anyone who steps foot in it will be cursed forever. I'm no' goin'."

"We're no' steppin' foot in the castle. Besides, it's too late to turn back," said Hawke with a chuckle. "Mayhap it's time for ye to face yer fear of all these silly superstitions."

"How is the castle haunted?" asked Phoebe.

"A woman was murdered and pushed from the tower," said Orrick. "It is said her ghost roams the castle as she looks for her murderer and tries to kill the man."

"Och, that's awful." Phoebe shuddered. "I hope we're no' goin' anywhere near it."

"We'll be close enough to see it," said Orrick.

"Perhaps we'll even see and hear the ghost," said Hawke, chuckling as he steered the boat, watching Ethan stir restlessly on the seat.

HAWKE HAD FIGURED Phoebe was going to try to go to the isle and that is why he'd decided to sleep on his boat. The wench was persistent and he knew she'd never give up. He figured the best thing to do was to take her there himself, and not risk her getting hurt, or possibly wrecking his boat.

This was going to slow him down and keep him from sleeping when he needed to be prepared to sneak in to the MacNabs' castle and rescue his grandda in the morning. He could have refused to take her and locked her up so she couldn't go. But he didn't. Something inside him wanted to please her. He loved seeing how excited she got and he also wanted to help her. After seeing what Euan MacNab did to her siblings, he was sure her father was in worse shape than they thought. That is, if he was even still alive at all.

Phoebe was right. She needed the herbs to help heal her father. Because if Angus MacNab didn't recover and take back his castle soon, there would never be reconciliation between the clans. Without him as chieftain, there would be no alliance, ever.

"We're here," said Phoebe when they approached the isle. Ethan hopped out of the boat to help dock at the shore and his dog followed, splashing around in the water.

"That mutt better dry off before she gets back in the boat," warned Hawke. Just as he said that, Trapper shook water all over him. Hawke grumbled and walked away.

"Follow me," Orrick told the others as they ventured onto the isle in the dark. He pulled a small lantern out of his bag. Hawke wasn't sure how he lit it, but wouldn't be surprised if he'd used magic. Right now, he didn't even care. He just wanted to quickly find the plants and return to camp so he could continue his mission.

It was a slight trek to find the herbs they needed but, soon enough, Orrick stopped and pointed to plants with small purplish clusters of flowers covering the ground.

"Here we go," he said with a wide smile, seeming just as excited as Phoebe to find the damned plants that Hawke was sure were really weeds.

"All right, quickly collect what ye need and let's go," said Hawke.

"Be sure to get the entire plants," Orrick told Phoebe as they started to pick them and fill up a large burlap bag that Orrick had with him. "Every part of the Common Centaury plant is healing. Plus, it makes a good tincture when boiled that is good for the organs and inner problems."

"That's exactly what my faither needs," said Phoebe, collecting the herbs with a smile on her face.

All of a sudden, they heard the sound of a woman screaming. Hawke's hand shot to his sword and he and Ethan both had their weapons drawn in a second.

"What was that?" asked Ethan, looking across the field. The moon broke through the clouds, illuminating a castle in the distance.

"Look! That must be the haunted castle," said Phoebe, pointing to it.

"Aye," agreed Orrick. "That it is. Ever since the murder there, the ghost appears and everyone avoids this isle."

"The ghost," said Ethan, turning white. "We should go now."

"Damn it, Ethan, ye are actin' like a scared wench," Hawke told him. "There is no such thing as a ghost."

"Then what's that?" Ethan pointed to a figure emerging from the woods. Trapper growled and took off at a run after it.

"It looks like a woman in a long cape," said Phoebe.

"Let's get back to the boat and leave this cursed place," said Ethan, acting like a scared fool again.

"I think we have more than enough herbs to last a long time," Orrick told them.

"Then let's go," agreed Phoebe.

"Nay. I'm no' goin' anywhere until I prove to Ethan that it is no' a ghost." Hawke took off at a run, following the path the wolfhound had taken. He followed the barking of the dog. When he broke through the clearing, he saw a frightened woman in a tangle of clothes, sitting on the ground with her hands over her head to protect her.

"Lass, it's all right," Hawke told her.

"Trapper, back down," shouted Ethan as he and the others ran up behind him.

"Give me yer hand," said Hawke, shoving his sword back into its sheath and reaching out for the mysterious woman. The girl slowly uncovered her head and looked up at Hawke. The moon bathed her pale face and sunken eyes.

Hawke's body froze as the woman took his hand. "Nay, it canna be so," he mumbled.

"What's goin' on?" asked Phoebe, pushing to the front to see the girl. Her eyes settled on the woman and her mouth fell open. "Osla," she said. "Ye are alive!"

"Osla?" asked Orrick in question.

"Aye," answered Phoebe. "Osla is my cousin."

"And Hawke's wife," added Ethan.

CHAPTER 21

Hawke felt numb as he helped Osla to her feet. How could this be? He saw her lying on the ground, dead, with one of his arrows sticking out of her back. None of this made any sense.

"Osla," he said, her name sounding foreign on his tongue. "I dinna understand. How are ye still alive? And what are ye doin' here?"

There was another scream from the castle, taking all their attentions.

"Canna we discuss this back at the boat?" asked Ethan.

"Of course we can," said Phoebe, wrapping her arm around Osla's shoulders. "Come on, Cousin. Ye are comin' back with us."

"Who are ye and where are we goin'?" asked Osla, sounding frightened.

"Osla, it's me, Phoebe. What is the matter that ye dinna remember me? And this is Hawke – yer husband."

"Nay," said the girl, shaking her head. Her gaze seemed distant, as if she were in a dream world. "My husband is Euan."

"God's eyes, what is goin' on here?" growled Hawke.

"I suggest we get back to the MacKeefe camp where we'll be safe," said Orrick. "We can figure this out there."

"I agree." Phoebe started to lead her cousin away.

"Nay! I willna leave without my children," cried the woman.

"What?" asked Phoebe. "Osla, are ye sayin' ye have children?"

"Aye. Oliver, Sophie, come here," called Osla. Two children shot out from the dark, running to their mother. "Oliver is nine and Sophie is six," she told them.

"Osla, I think we have a lot of things to talk about," said Phoebe. "But first, Cousin, let's get ye and yer children to safety."

The old sorcerer, the girls, and the children headed back to the boat, led by Trapper.

"Hawke? What's happen' here?" asked Ethan in confusion.

"I dinna ken, but I intend to find out soon." Hawke looked back over his shoulder at the foreboding castle behind them, starting to wonder exactly what kind of place this was. "I'm startin' to get a bad feelin' about all this," said Hawke.

"Startin' to?" Ethan's brows dipped. "I told ye we shouldna have come here. This isle is cursed I tell ye. This should prove it. Yer dead wife has come back from the grave."

"I'm no' so sure about that," said Hawke, walking back to the boat. "But findin' out that Osla is still alive is goin' to prove to be a curse on me for sure."

"What do ye mean?" asked Ethan, walking with him at a brisk pace. "I thought ye'd be happy that yer wife didna die after all."

"Egads, Ethan, what do ye think I mean? Dinna ye realize the predicament I'm in? I've fallen in love with Phoebe. But now – now I canna even think of possibly marryin' her someday because I'm already married to a woman I dinna love and who I thought was dead. I'm no' sure why Osla thinks Euan is her husband, and I have no idea who sired her children. However, I'm pretty sure Euan is behind everythin', probably havin' done somethin' to fake her death so the feud would continue."

"Aye, that's a problem," agreed Ethan. He looked over his

shoulder once again at the castle and shook his head. "This place is haunted and cursed, Hawke. I swear I just saw the ghost of the dead woman watchin' me from the tower window."

"Ye're imaginin' it, Ethan."

"Even so, I never want to come back here as long as I live."

* * *

"Osla, I am so happy to see ye," said Phoebe, hugging her cousin as the boat headed back for the MacKeefe camp. "I thought ye were dead. How is it ye are still alive? And have children?"

"Phoebe," said the girl, seeming to think hard about her name. "I vaguely remember someone named Phoebe."

"Osla, we were like sisters," said Phoebe, grabbing the girl's hands in hers. "Why dinna ye remember me?"

"How long have ye been on the isle?" asked Hawke.

"I – I dinna ken," she told them. "Euan would ken. We should wait here for him to return. He'll answer all yer questions. Ye see, I have a hard time rememberin' things." Her body shook and Phoebe wasn't sure if it was from the cold or from fear.

Phoebe removed her cloak and put it around her cousin. "Are ye hungry?" she asked the poor children who looked tired and dirty and very skinny.

"Aye," said the boy. The little girl didn't talk at all. They both looked frightened.

"I think I have some leftover bread in my pouch," said Orrick, pulling out half a loaf that Phoebe hadn't even known he had. He handed it to the children.

"Thank ye," said the boy taking the bread and breaking off a piece for his sister and mother before he ate.

"I'm so tired," said Osla, her eyes closing as she held the cloak tightly around her.

"We dinna need to talk tonight," said Phoebe. "Once we get

back to the MacKeefe Clan, ye'll all get more food and ale and pallets to sleep on," Phoebe told them.

"MacKeefe?" asked the boy, his eyes going from Hawke to Ethan and back to her. "My father told me the MacKeefes are our enemies and no guid." He took another bite of bread. "He said if we ever see one we should kill them."

"Nay, that's no' right," said Phoebe. "Hawke and Ethan here are MacKeefes and they are guid people, I assure ye."

"Why are ye with them?" asked the boy, looking at her plaid. "Are ye a MacNab?"

"Aye, I am," she said with a nod. "I'm with them because I am their . . . prisoner."

"And are we prisoners of the MacKeefes, too?" the boy persisted.

"Nay, ye are no' our prisoners and neither is Phoebe," said Hawke.

Phoebe looked up at Hawke in surprise. "I'm no'?" she asked.

"Well . . . no' really." Hawke busied himself with the rudder as they left the island. "No more talkin'. There's too much noise. I dinna want to hear another word on our trip back."

"Aye, we're prisoners," the boy told his sister, pulling the little girl closer to him. It about broke Phoebe's heart.

CHAPTER 22

Hawke sat by the fire, thinking, after Phoebe had taken Osla and her children back to the infirmary to sleep. Orrick had gone with him. Things were going from bad to worse and Hawke didn't know what to do.

"So, I dinna understand," said Caleb, lounging back against a log with a bowl of berries next to him. "I thought yer wife was dead." He popped a bilberry into his mouth.

"For ten years!" said Logan, sitting on a log next to Caleb on one side while Ethan was on the other. Ethan's dog was sprawled out on the ground sleeping. Logan's wolf spotted something in the dark and took off at a run.

"And she has children," said Ethan, taking a swig of Mountain Magic. "She also said her husband was Euan. The lass seems very confused."

"How old would ye say her boy is?" Logan took a swig of Mountain Magic as well.

"I believe she said the boy was nine and the girl was six," said Ethan.

"Nine, huh?" Logan smacked his lips together, savoring the taste of the whisky.

"Dinna even say it, Logan, because I ken what ye're thinkin'," said Hawke, feeling worse than ever.

"What? What is he thinkin'?" Caleb popped another berry into his mouth.

"Since he was married to Osla that the boy might be his," Ethan answered for him.

"Really?" Caleb sat up. "Do ye think ye have a child?"

"I dinna ken what to think," said Hawke. "We were only married for a short time, but I suppose he could be mine. I dinna ken." Hawke broke off a piece of a twig and threw it into the fire.

"If the wench canna even remember bein' married to ye, then I doubt the boy is yers," said Ethan.

"Aye, why canna she remember?" Caleb reached down for another berry, finding the bowl empty. "Och, who stole my berries? Logan, was it ye?"

"Me? I dinna even like berries," said Logan, making a face.

"Ethan?" Caleb turned and glared at his other friend sitting beside him.

"Dinna look at me. I'm drinkin' Mountain Magic. It doesna go with berries."

"Then where are they? I had an entire bowl of them."

"Ye're just as addled as that wench," said Logan, raising his tankard to his mouth. All of a sudden, his eyes opened wide and he jumped up off the log. "Bid the devil, somethin' just brushed past my leg."

Trapper's head popped up, but the dog stayed lying down, yawning.

"What's the matter with ye two?" asked Hawke. "Ye're actin' like scared lassies, just like Ethan did when we got too close to the castle on the isle."

"It's haunted, I tell ye," said Ethan. Then he jumped up as well. "Somethin' brushed by my leg, too."

"Mayhap it was a ghost," said Hawke sarcastically, throwing the twig into the fire.

"Nay, it's no'. Look," said Caleb, pointing in the dark. "It's some kind of critter that is stealin' my food."

Trapper let out a low growl and finally got up and took off after the bandit animal, followed by Caleb as they ran through the camp.

"Do ye think Euan is really married to her and the faither of her children?" asked Logan.

"I dinna ken what to think," said Hawke, getting to his feet as well. "But I plan on findin' out." He headed toward the stable.

"Wait. Where are ye goin'?" asked Ethan.

"I'm goin' to Crookston Castle to confront Euan. I get a feelin' he's been makin' a fool of me, and I will no' let that go unpunished."

"But what about Ian? I thought we were goin' to save our chieftain," said Logan, following after him.

"The plans just changed," said Hawke, furious to even think of Euan bedding his wife. "I'm goin' to find out the truth and then I'm goin' to kill Euan for what he's done."

"Hawke, wait! Slow down," said Ethan. "Ye're no' thinkin' straight. Ye canna just walk in and kill the man!"

"Then I'll sneak in and strangle the truth out of him and then I'll kill him, collect Ian, and be back before sunup."

"Ye're bein' a fool," said Logan. "At least let us come with ye."

"Nay. We've got more MacNabs here now than I want. If word of this gets out, we might just have MacNab warriors at our door. Stay here and watch over the lassies and the children."

"We've got other men here to do that," said Logan. "I'm comin' with ye."

"Nay!" Hawke said, spinning around on his heel, angrier than hell. "I need time alone and with ye three along, I will never be able to collect my thoughts." Hawke quickly saddled his horse and pulled himself up. "And whatever ye do, do no', I repeat, do no', let Phoebe out of yer sight. The last thing I want is for her to do somethin' stupid."

"She's no' the one we're worried about," mumble Ethan into his mug. Hawke took off into the night, heading for the MacNabs to settle things once and for all.

* * *

PHOEBE WATCHED from the door of the infirmary as Hawke rode away into the night. She'd heard every word the men said, and she didn't like this in the least.

"Phoebe? Are ye comin' back to bed?" asked Osla, walking up behind her.

"Osla, dinna ye remember bein' married to Hawke?" asked Phoebe, still staring out the door.

"Nay," she said, rubbing her head. "Well, mayhap. I'm no' sure. I had a bad fall off the side of a cliff about ten years ago. Euan told me I was close to death because I hit my head. I have trouble rememberin' anythin' from my past, but Euan has been helpin' me."

"Aye, he's helpin' ye remember but only what he wants ye to believe."

"What do ye mean, Phoebe?" Osla yawned and pushed a long lock of hair behind her ear.

"Osla, the MacNabs and MacKeefes have been feudin' for years. Ye were married to Hawke for an alliance. But supposedly, ye died on a hunt and the MacNabs blamed Hawke for it and the feud continued."

"I'm sorry, Phoebe, but I really dinna remember."

"Is Euan really married to ye?"

"Aye. Or, at least that is what he told me. Do ye think he lied?"

"I'm willin' to bet on it." Phoebe turned to face her. "Why does he keep ye and the children on a haunted isle while he lives back at Crookston Castle?"

"Crookston?" she asked, as if she'd never heard the name.

"It's the MacNabs' castle, Osla. I dinna understand why ye are bein' hidden away on an isle that no one goes to. No' unless Euan doesna want the rest of the clan to ken ye're alive."

"Euan told me he wanted to protect me. The children and I live in a little hut on the isle and we tend the sheep for the laird of the castle. It's a guid life, Phoebe. I dinna mind."

"It's also a lie, Osla. Ye are Hawke's wife." She wiped a tear from her eye.

"Why are ye cryin'?" asked Osla. "Is it because ye wish ye were Hawke's wife instead?"

Phoebe jolted in surprise. Her cousin's mind might be addled and her memories of the past all gone, but she was still sharp enough that she could see Phoebe had feelings for Hawke.

"I have fallen in love with him, Cousin." Phoebe held back the tears. "And now I ken that I will never be able to be his wife, because ye already are."

"But I dinna even ken him," she protested. "I dinna want him for my husband. I have Euan. He's the one I love."

"If ye kent what Euan is really like, ye would hate him, the same as me."

"What are ye sayin', Phoebe?" Confusion covered the girl's face.

"Osla, the reason we were on the island was to collect herbs to heal my faither. He is sick and dyin' and Euan has claimed the castle as his own. He's just waitin' for my faither to die. I wouldna be surprised if he already killed him."

"Nay, Euan would never do that," said Osla, obviously shaken.

"He would, Osla. He imprisoned my sisters and brathair. If Hawke hadna saved them, they would have died in the dungeon."

"Euan put women and a child in the dungeon?" Osla seemed horrified by the thought.

"Euan is no' the man ye think he is. And I'm sorry to say, he's taken advantage of ye. Yer whole life is a lie." Phoebe headed out the door.

"Wait! Where are ye goin', Phoebe?"

"I'm goin' after Hawke to try to keep him from bein' killed," she told her cousin. Then she looked down and patted the bag slung over her shoulder. "I'm also goin' to heal my faither with the herbs I collected, so he can take back his castle and things can be made right again."

"But ye are one woman. What can ye do?"

Phoebe bent down and checked her throwing knives – her only protection. "I have to try," she told Osla.

"Then let me come with ye."

"Nay. Ye stay here and watch over yer children and also my siblin's. Please."

"All right," agreed Osla, sounding dejected. "Whatever ye say, Phoebe."

Phoebe slipped through the shadows, avoiding Hawke's friends who were looking up a tree while the wolfhound barked at something. It was her perfect opportunity to slip away in the dark. She made her way to the stable to get a horse and follow Hawke. Phoebe would not let the man she loved die without trying to do something to remedy this horrible situation.

* * *

HAWKE SHIMMIED the wall of Crookston Castle with his dagger clenched between his teeth. His blood boiled and he no longer cared how dangerous the mission was. He was going to put an end to this immediately. No more waiting to negotiate, no more letting more people die. Euan and his men would be stopped and Hawke would save his grandfather. Now, if only he had a plan.

Figuring his grandfather was being imprisoned in one of the tower rooms, he'd brought with him a grappling hook and rope. It seemed their guards were scarce and he hoped most of them had gone to help fight the English on the coast. If so, this would be easy.

Choosing a tower, he started to climb, hoping this was the right one.

After making it to the top, he gripped his fingers on the edge of the sill and pulled himself up and over the window, landing with a soft thump inside the room.

"Grandda," he called out softly, trying to see in the dark. The sun had just started to rise but the room was dim with no candle burning or fire on the hearth. "Grandda are ye in here?"

He took two steps into the room and stopped in his tracks. A man lay on the bed without moving. He was either sleeping . . . or dead. Hawk slowly walked up to the bed, hoping not to find his chieftain murdered. He let out a sigh of relief when he realized it wasn't his grandfather, but rather the MacNab chieftain. It was Phoebe's sick father, Angus.

The man looked thin and pale, and near death. He appeared very different from how Hawke remembered him from ten years ago when he'd married Osla. Angus' eyes were closed and his cheeks looked hollow as the first rays of sun hit him in the face from the open window. This wasn't why Hawke was here. There was nothing he could do to help this man. He turned to leave, but stopped when he heard a faint voice from the bed.

"Hawke. Is that ye?"

He turned around, not sure what to say to the man. "Aye," he answered, feeling choked up.

"Is – is my daughter . . . alive?"

Suddenly, Hawke felt no better than Euan. For all this man knew, Hawke could have killed Phoebe. After all, he was her captor.

"She is safe," he told the man, walking closer to the bed. He wanted to give him hope if he could. "I took her to the Isle of Kerrera to get herbs. To cure ye," he added. "She'll bring ye back to health."

"Please, dinna hurt her. She means everythin' to me."

"Nay, I would never hurt her," he tried to convince the man to put his mind at ease. Hawke pulled up a chair and sat down for a moment at the side of the bed. The least he could do is to tell him about his daughter so he could die in peace. "I love Phoebe, Laird Angus. I promise I will take care of her, even long after ye are gone."

God's teeth, he didn't mean to make it sound so bad. He was trying to get the man's mind off of dying, but that probably didn't help any.

"I've also saved yer other children, Miles, Elspeth and Agan from the dungeon."

"The dungeon?" The man tried to push up in bed, but coughed and lay back down and moaned. "Euan did it, didna he?"

"Aye, he did." Hawke hesitated for a minute, but then he thought he should let the man know everything. "We found yer niece, Osla, on the island. It seems Euan is her husband and they have two children together. She canna remember a thing from the past."

"God forgive me for no' stoppin' this madness sooner."

"What do ye mean?" asked Hawke, leaning in closer to hear what the man said. "Did ye ken she was still alive?" He seriously hoped Angus had nothing to do with this deception.

"I have been hearin' rumors for years now that Osla wasna dead and that someone faked her death to keep the feud between our clans goin' strong. But I didna believe it. I guess I didna want to think that any of my men could be such traitors."

"It's Euan. And Lennox," Hawke told him. "Mayhap more."

"I ken that now. Euan has taken everythin' from me. I canna let him do this. Stop him, Highland Storm."

"Highland Storm?" Hawke asked in confusion. "Nay, Laird Angus, that is no' me. The Highland Storm is my faither."

"Ye are his son. I'm sure ye will follow in his footsteps. Do it. Rid us of these traitors."

"But wouldna that cause more problems between the clans?"

"We have an alliance," said the man. "Ye are married to a MacNab."

"Aye, but it seems Euan has claimed Osla for his wife. Besides, I dinna want her. I would rather be married to Phoebe."

"Do ye really mean that, Hawke?" came a voice from the door.

Hawke jumped up with his sword drawn, spinning around to find Phoebe standing in the doorway.

"Phoebe! Bid the devil, what are ye doin' here? Ye are supposed to be back at the MacKeefe camp bein' guarded by Caleb, Logan, and Ethan. I should have kent I couldna rely on them."

"Och, that," she said with a giggle. "Dinna be angry with yer friends. I snuck out when they were busy chasin' some critter up a tree."

"Phoebe, it's no' safe. Ye shouldna be here," Hawke warned her.

"This is my home, Hawke. I need to be here because I want to heal my faither."

"Intruders!" shouted someone from out in the courtyard.

"Now what?" mumbled Hawke, running to look out the window. "God's eyes, nay," he said, seeing Osla and Orrick riding in on horses over the drawbridge.

"Who is it?" asked Phoebe, coming up behind him. "Oh, nay," she said.

"Ye didna by any chance tell Osla where ye were goin', did ye?" asked Hawke.

"I might have mentioned it," she answered shyly. "I'm sorry, I didna think she'd even remember how to get here since her memories seem to be gone."

"That's probably why she brought Orrick. Now stay here with yer faither because all hell is about to break loose and I dinna want ye around when I'm fightin'."

"Hawke, nay!" cried Phoebe as he hurried to the door. "Ye canna fight them all by yerself. Ye'll be slaughtered."

"Where is my grandda?" Hawke asked Angus.

"I believe they are keepin' him in the solar next to the great hall," said the man, closing his eyes partially. "Come here, Daughter, so I can say guidbye."

"I willna let ye die, Da," said Phoebe, pulling the herbs out of her travel bag. Hawke wanted to stay there now and help Phoebe cure her father. If the man died, Hawke didn't want Phoebe there alone. But now he had no choice. He had to find his grandfather and, hopefully, the two of them could fight their way out of there.

He turned around and ran down the corridor, heading for the solar by the great hall. Breaking into the room, he found his grandfather tied up on the bed.

"Grandda," he said, rushing to the man's side and slashing the ropes to set him free. "Are ye hurt?"

"I've been better," said Ian, rubbing his wrists. "What took ye so long to get me, Hawke? And where the hell is Storm?"

"The English are invadin' and Da and some of the others went to fight with the Scots," he told him. "But right now, we have to fight Euan and his men if we're goin' to get out of here alive."

"Get my sword, Hawke. They put it in the trunk by the window."

Hawke quickly got Ian's sword and helped him from the bed. The man was weak and tired and had been mistreated. It was hard for him even to stand.

"On second thought, ye'd better stay here, Grandda. I dinna think ye are in any shape to fight. I'll be back." Hawke turned and ran from the room. When he approached the courtyard, he saw Euan holding his sword up to Orrick.

"Let him go," cried Hawke, making his presence known.

"MacKeefe!" Euan kept his blade at Orrick's chest and turned enough to talk to Hawke. "Ye must want to die if ye came here by yerself."

"Who said he's here by himself?" Ethan appeared from the shadows with his wolfhound at his side. The hound growled and showed its teeth, keeping its head low. Hawke heard Apollo's screech and looked up to see his bird landing on the merlon of the battlement.

Euan chuckled. "Ye think two of ye is enough to fight me and my clan?"

"Make that three," called out Caleb from up on the battlements.

"Four," said Logan, riding over the drawbridge, being led by his wolf.

"Ye all have a death wish, dinna ye?" asked Euan.

Hawke's friends looked over to him for the command to attack, but Hawke held his hand up in the air. "Euan, ye bluidy cur, tell me what ye've done to Osla."

"Ye are such a fool, MacKeefe," snapped Euan. "It's been ten years and yet ye never discovered that Osla didna die." He chuckled lowly at his cunning trick.

"I saw her at the bottom of the cliff with an arrow in her back and lots of bluid." Hawke walked closer to Euan with his sword leading the way.

"Careful, Euan," said Lennox, turning his back to Euan, looking around him with his sword held high. A few more of Euan's loyal men did the same. "They're surroundin' us."

"I'm no' afraid of a few MacKeefes," snapped Euan. "Hawke, it was so easy that it still amuses me to this day," he bragged, relaying his story. "I stole one of yer arrows, pushed Osla down the hill, and then hit her over the head just to knock her out. Then I hid a dead bird under her clothes with the arrow piercin' it, no' her. I convinced the clan, and of course ye, that ye'd killed her. Afterward, I took her to the isle where no one ever goes so she'd be mine. I thought I'd have to force her to couple with me, but the knock over the head made her forget everythin' and it was easier than I ever thought."

"Then, ye're no' my husband, Euan?" asked Osla.

"Nay, ye're just my bitch. I never married ye. I just wanted ye because ye were MacKeefe's."

"Ye bastard!" Hawke took a step forward, but a hand on his arm stopped him.

"Easy, Hawke," said Ian. "Ye've got a temper like yer faither's. Dinna let them goad ye into a fight."

"Grandda, my da told me ye were the one always wantin' to fight, no' him."

"Things have changed over the years, Hawke. Now all I want is peace between the clans."

"I willna make peace with Euan or the like."

"Nay, but think of their laird dyin' up in the tower. Do it for him and for his family."

Hawke didn't want peace. He wanted to see Euan, Lennox and the rest of them dead for imprisoning old men, women and children. Still, he had to try. For Phoebe's sake.

"What will it take, MacNab?" asked Hawke. "What do ye want for our clans to make an alliance?"

"I was goin' to ask for a high ransom. But since the MacKeefes probably wouldna be able to pay, I decided I want somethin' else instead. I want to be laird of the MacNabs and I want the MacKeefes to give me Hermitage Castle."

"What? Never!" shouted Ian. "I'll kill ye if ye even think of tryin' to take that away."

Now it was Hawke who had to hold back his grandfather from fighting.

"Euan, look who I found in the tower!" One of Euan's men dragged Phoebe out into the courtyard. He held her hands behind her back.

"Phoebe," cried Hawke. "Nay. Dinna touch her!" He rushed forward, but Euan reached out and grabbed Phoebe, holding her tightly to his body and putting the blade against her throat.

"Give me Hermitage Castle, or I'll kill her," said Euan. "Simple as that."

"She's one of yer own, ye fool," laughed Ian. "Go ahead and kill her, what do we care?"

"Nay!" shouted Hawke, turning to look at his grandfather. "I love her, Grandda. I would die for her."

"Blethers, Hawke! Haud yer wheesht," spat Ian through gritted teeth. "Now that they ken that, we have no chance at all."

"Leave me alone," shouted Phoebe, stomping on Euan's foot and elbowing him in the gut, pushing away. Hawke rushed forward, but was blocked by three men.

"Get them," shouted Hawke, giving his friends the command to step in. Ian fought at his side and a melee broke out.

PHOEBE LOOKED up to see Euan with fire in his eyes, coming right for her.

"Ye bitch! I should have kent that ye'd only be trouble and killed ye years ago. If MacKeefe loves ye so much, then I think ye have to die."

"Nay!" she cried, scooting backward on the ground as Euan lunged for her. Hawke was fighting off three men and neither he nor his friends could help her. But as Euan's blade lashed out, Osla dove in front of her to stop him.

"Dinna hurt my cousin, Euan!" she cried, taking the sword in her chest to save Phoebe.

"Osla, ye fool!" Euan pulled his sword from her chest and her body crumpled to the ground.

"Euan, I'm goin' to kill ye," cried Hawke, taking down two men and coming for him. As they fought, Phoebe crawled over to Osla, crying and cradling her brave cousin in her arms.

"Osla, why did ye do that?" asked Phoebe.

"Phoebe, I remember," said Osla, a peaceful smile coming to

her face. "The fall must have jarred my memory and now I remember each and every awful thing Euan has done."

"Orrick," cried Phoebe. "Orrick come here, quickly." She held Osla as the blood poured from her wound. Phoebe used the end of her own gown to try to stop the flow.

"Take care . . . of my . . . children," said Osla, blood spurting from her wound as well as coming from her mouth. "Promise . . . me . . ."

"Aye, of course, I will," promised Phoebe, trying to force a smile to calm her dying cousin. "But ye will no' die, Osla. Orrick and I will heal ye. Orrick," she called out again, looking up to see Orrick with a sword, fighting just as well as any knight. This surprised her, since she never knew he had the skill. Especially since he was such an old man. When she looked back down at Osla, she realized the woman was dead. Tears streamed from Phoebe's eyes.

"Ye'll never hurt anyone again," cried Hawke, pushing his sword through Euan, managing to kill the man. But Phoebe noticed Lennox rushing toward Hawke. The man was atop a horse with two swords swinging as he rode up behind him. Hawke wouldn't be able to remove his sword from Euan and turn around fast enough to defend himself.

Reaching under her gown, Phoebe ripped her throwing knife from the sheath strapped to her leg and flung the blade across the courtyard, hitting Lennox in the back. He stiffened and dropped one sword, but continued to go after Hawke. Hawke realized what was happening, retrieved his sword and spun around, but not before Phoebe could throw the knife from her boot, hitting Lennox a second time. The man fell from the horse at Hawke's feet.

Hawke looked up at her in surprise and nodded his thanks.

"Stop this fightin', Hawke," she shouted. "No more killin', please. Osla is dead."

"Hold up, men," called out Hawke as Phoebe ran to him.

"MacNab Clan, stop fightin'. It's over," she cried, but the men didn't seem to listen to her.

Just when Phoebe thought all was lost, her father appeared on the battlements with Orrick, even though Phoebe had no idea how Orrick got up there so quickly.

"I speak for Laird MacNab," called out Orrick in a deep, booming voice. "He is near death and tells me it was because of Euan. He wants this fighting to stop and for the MacNabs and the MacKeefes to align."

The fighting slowed as Orrick continued.

"He is granting pardon to any of Euan's men who will drop their swords and pay allegiance to him again. Those who refuse will be imprisoned."

The sound of metal clanking to the ground echoed in the courtyard as man after man dropped their swords and bowed down on one knee to Angus, up on the battlements.

"It's done," shouted Hawke, so everyone could hear him. "The MacKeefes and the MacNabs from this day on will be allies instead of enemies. And to seal the alliance, I ask ye, Laird MacNab, for yer daughter's hand in marriage." Hawke held out his hand to Phoebe.

Orrick leaned over and listened to something Angus said, that could not be heard by everyone else.

"Laird Angus agrees to the marriage, since your former bride has just been killed by Euan," announced Orrick. "Hawke, you are free to marry her but only if Phoebe agrees."

"Aye. I want to marry Hawke, and I want our clans aligned," said Phoebe. "Too many needless deaths were brought upon our people and we'll have no more."

Phoebe walked over to Osla's dead body, kneeling down and kissing her cousin upon the head before gently closing the woman's eyes. There was nothing she could do for her cousin, but she might still be able to help her father.

"Phoebe, I'm so sorry about Osla," said Hawke, helping her up.

"Hawke, I love ye, but I canna talk to ye now. I have to try to heal my faither."

"Go," he said with a nod. "My friends and I will see to the dead. And I promise ye, nothin' like this will ever happen again between our clans."

"I love ye, Hawke. And I believe ye," she said, running off to help Orrick to try to heal her father before she lost him as well.

CHAPTER 23

Hawke rode back to the MacKeefe camp with Phoebe sitting in front on him on his horse. He wrapped his arms around her, never wanting to let her go. Leaning forward, he kissed her atop her head.

Ian rode with them and so did Ethan, followed by his hound. Orrick and Logan stayed at the MacNabs' castle for now. It had taken a good part of the day to bury the dead and clean up. Things were over now, but Hawke still felt unsettled.

"I am glad the herbs we collected from the isle are already helpin' my faither," said Phoebe. "Orrick said my faither will live, although his recovery will be slow."

"I am so happy for ye, Phoebe. And I am sorry about Osla."

"She dove in front of Euan's blade to protect me, Hawke. And because of it, she died."

"It was her choice, lass."

"I made her a promise when she was dyin', that I intend to carry out."

"Of course," he told her. "A promise to a dyin' person should never be broken."

"We're goin' to be raisin' her children as our own," she said, causing Hawke to go speechless.

PHOEBE WAITED for Hawke to respond, but he was much too quiet. "Hawke, did ye hear me?"

"I did," he finally answered.

"Well, what do ye think about the idea? We'll have an instant family even before we are married."

"I dinna like the idea of raisin' Euan's children, because I have a lot of hatred for the man."

"But they are also Osla's children, Hawke. Her boy is auld enough to be . . . to be yers from when ye were married to my cousin."

"I ken that, Phoebe. And it bothers me that the only two people who can give me the answer if Oliver is from my seed or not are dead."

"Does it matter?" she asked. "Raise him as if he were truly yers."

"I suppose."

"I talked to some of my faither's men who ken what happened with Osla," said Phoebe.

"I heard what Euan confessed."

"Aye. I guess it started out as a plot to frame ye and keep the feud goin' between our clans. My faither had nothin' to do with it. Euan carried it out, and then hid Osla on the Isle of Kerrera because it was said to be haunted. He was sure no one would go there except for the people who lived there."

"I canna believe what a fool I was to no' have kent about this for ten long years."

"No one but a few of Euan's men were aware of it. No' even my faither. I also learned that even though he wouldna admit it aloud, Euan really did care for Osla. That is why he kept it a secret so long. It worked in his favor since she hit her head and lost her memory. He could tell her anythin' and she'd believe it."

"Well, it's over now, lass. And I am no' lookin' forward to tellin' Osla's children that they lost both of their parents."

"I'll do that," offered Phoebe. "And think of it this way – they'll have two new parents now."

"And someday, we'll have more bairns of our own makin'."

"Of course we will. Hawke, tell me somethin', honestly."

"What is it, lass?"

"If Osla were still alive . . . would ye have lived with her since ye were still married to her? After all, we couldna be married if ye already took yer vows with my cousin."

"I love ye, Phoebe. I would have found any way possible to marry ye. Besides, after ten years, and by the fact she had children with another man, I am sure we could have convinced the church to give me an annulment."

Caleb rode by on his horse, cradling something in his arms.

"Wait," Hawke called out, his low voice vibrating against her back. "What have ye got there, Caleb?"

"Only the little critter that kept stealin' my food. I've decided since he willna leave me alone, he'll be my new pet." He held up something that looked like a cross between a weasel and a polecat.

"What is it?" asked Phoebe, not sure she'd ever seen anything like it before.

"It's a pine marten," he told her. "It's usually nocturnal so it's sleepin' now. It likes to snuggle up in my travel bag." He reached down and put the slinky animal into the bag attached to his horse.

"Yer pet is a pine marten?" asked Hawke. "How is that supposed to help ye or scare away intruders?"

"Its stealth is what I admire the most," said Caleb. "I'm goin' to teach it to be a little thief. Then, when I need somethin' from an enemy . . . or possibly even ye, I'll send in Marty to get it."

"Oh, ye named it Marty. How cute," said Phoebe with a giggle.

"I think it's ridiculous," grumbled Hawke. "But then again, I'd expect no less from ye, Caleb."

Apollo shrieked from up in the sky and Hawke held out his arm. The bird landed in a flutter of wings. Phoebe jerked, not feeling comfortable near the bird yet.

"What is that in its mouth?" she asked.

"Looks like Apollo picked up a mouse for lunch."

"A mouse! Get it away from me," she cried.

"Go on, Apollo," said Hawke, sending his bird up into the sky.

"So when's the weddin' and where will it be?" asked Ian, riding up to talk with them.

"I dinna ken," said Hawke. "I suppose wherever Phoebe wants it."

"I'd like it to take place at the MacKeefe camp in the Highlands," she told him.

"Are ye sure?" asked Hawke. "It might be better to house and feed all the people from both clans at either Crookston or Hermitage Castle."

"Nay. I'd prefer it out in nature. And I'd like to have a mini Highland Feis as well, where the MacNabs and the MacKeefes can compete."

"The Highland Feis doesna take place until the fall," said Caleb.

"And they are for all the clans, no' just two," added Ian.

"Well, this will be our special gatherin'," said Phoebe. "A Highland Feis Weddin' Celebration. I want to see Hawke toss the caber again."

"Hah!" said Ian. "He can toss it, but my son, Storm, will win. He always does."

"Well, mayhap it's time to change that because, this time, I am goin' to win," said Hawke, sounding mighty confidant.

"If so, we'd better make sure that the king's chronicler and his daughter attend so they can record the deed," suggested Phoebe.

"Och, no' them," complained Hawke.

"Why no'?" asked Phoebe. "Afraid ye're goin' to lose?"

"Nay. I just dinna want to see Caleb followin' that wench around like a lovesick lad again."

"I dinna do that," protested Caleb.

"Ye are obsessed with that lass for some reason," said Hawke.

"Her name is Bridget and I am no' obsessed. However, she is very bonnie." A smile lit up Caleb's face and he shrugged. "I find her . . . mysterious."

"The only lass I care about is Phoebe," said Hawke, kissing her atop the head again. "And I canna wait to make ye my wife, my love."

CHAPTER 24

A SENNIGHT LATER

Phoebe walked forward, holding on to the arm of her father through the crowd of MacNabs and MacKeefes that joined together at the MacKeefe camp in the Highlands for her wedding to Hawke.

It was hard for Hawke to wait, but she'd convinced him that she wanted to postpone the wedding until her father was well enough to give her away. Angus MacNab was far from healed, but at least now he wasn't so weak and could walk on his own. They also waited until the men returned from the encounter with the English.

By the time the English made their way up to Edinburgh, the Scots had managed to hold off fighting by burning everything in sight. They were planning an ambush if the English decided to force them into the Highlands, but that never happened. The English turned back and all of the MacKeefes thankfully came home alive.

The Common Centaury and Hart's Tongue proved to make

the perfect tonic that Phoebe's father needed to heal. Phoebe proudly wore the purple and green plaid of the MacKeefes with a bright white tunic with ruffled sleeves. Her sisters, Elspeth and Agan, held baskets, scattering flower petals along her path all the way down to the water where Hawke waited with the others.

He looked so handsome in his plaid and with his long hair lifting in the breeze. Even though Phoebe and Hawke had already made love, she somehow felt nervous about sharing the wedding bed with him.

With the MacNabs on one side and the MacKeefes on the other, Phoebe and Hawke took their wedding vows. Then Orrick stepped forward with a strip of the MacKeefe plaid and a strip of the MacNab plaid held high for everyone to see.

"Hold out your hands," said Orrick, wrapping the strips around them in a handfasting ceremony that would join the two clans as one. When they were finished, they slipped their hands out of the strips of cloth and Orrick held up the knot entwined by both the plaids for everyone to see.

Cheers and shouts went up from the crowd, but then the priest asked for the rings.

"Caleb, give me the rings," Hawke said in a low voice while Ian and Logan looked on. Ethan stood to the side, holding his bagpipes.

"The rings," said Caleb, patting his pockets and then his pouch. "I had them right here." Hawke noticed a brown bushy tail disappearing under the table.

"Marty, ye thief, bring those rings back here," said Caleb, diving for the pine marten. Ethan's wolfhound thought it was a game, jumping on top of Caleb, knocking over the table. Then, when Jack, Logan's wolf, saw the pine marten running away, it took off after it in a mad dash.

"Nay, get back here, Jack," cried Logan, running after the wolf. "Dinna eat Caleb's pet."

"Forget the rings, we'll get them later," Hawke announced. "Everyone, back to the huts for a dram of whisky."

He leaned over and kissed Phoebe, making her giggle. She held a bouquet of flowers that he almost smashed.

"Throw the flowers," said little Sophie. She was happy with Hawke and Phoebe as her new parents, but Oliver scowled from the shadows, not yet accepting them since he'd heard that both Phoebe and Hawke were the ones to kill his father. But with time, Phoebe was sure he would come around, since he'd also heard that Euan was the one who killed his mother. Life was hard in the Highlands, and the events and situations often caused boys to turn to men quickly.

"Och, I almost forgot," said Phoebe, looking over her shoulder at her sisters, giving them the signal that she was going to throw the bouquet to Sophie. She threw it right to the little girl, but Phoebe's brother, Miles, jumped in front of her, catching it and running away.

"Give them to me," pouted the little girl, running after him.

"I think mayhap if we'd had the weddin' in a castle, there might have been a little less chaos," said Hawke.

"I dinna mind. I like it," said Phoebe, beaming with happiness. "It is a guid feelin' to have lots and lots of family."

"Hawke, I found the bag, but the rings must have rolled out," said Caleb, running up to them out of breath and slapping the torn silk bag into Hawke's hand.

"What am I supposed to do with this?" growled Hawke, throwing the bag to the ground. "Now, go find the rings."

"Right away," said Caleb, taking off at a run. Apollo screeched from the sky as everyone headed from the water's edge toward the main part of camp. The place was decorated beautifully with arches made of twisted branches and covered with Highland flowers such mountain avens, primrose and heather. There were a good half-dozen fires burning with lamb and pheasant roasting on spits. Tables were set up, covered in cloth of both the MacKeefe and the MacNab plaids. And lining each table were many jugs of old Callum MacKeefe's Mountain Magic.

Ethan followed Hawke and Phoebe, playing the bagpipes, stopping right behind them.

"Thank ye, that is beautiful," said Phoebe, but Hawke was less enthused.

"That's enough," he said, causing Ethan to stop playing.

"It's important to have bagpipes at yer weddin' to ward away any evil spirits," said Ethan.

"The only spirits here, I assure ye, are no' evil," Hawke told them, nodding to the Mountain Magic.

Hawke's sister, Heather, walked up with his older sister, Lark.

"Congratulations," they said, giving Hawke kisses on his cheeks and also hugging Phoebe.

"Out of the way," came the gruff old voice of Callum. "Hawke, ye need a little of my Mountain Magic to seal the weddin' vows." He handed Hawke a two-handled wooden cup. Hawke grabbed it with one hand, because his other hand was around Phoebe.

"Nay!" Ethan's eyes opened wide. "Ye need to hold the weddin' cup with two hands, or did ye forget?"

"What does it matter?" asked Hawke.

"Hawke, you know better," said his mother, Wren, pushing through the crowd. "It symbolizes the two clans joining as one."

"That's right," agreed Phoebe. "With both hands on the cup, it shows the other clan ye are no' holdin' a weapon."

"God's teeth, it is my weddin' day, of course I'm no' holdin' a weapon," complained Hawke. "I'm holdin' my wife." He leaned over and kissed Phoebe on the mouth again.

Ethan cleared his throat. "Dinna tempt the fates on yer weddin' day, Hawke. Follow tradition."

Hawke was about to object, when Phoebe stopped him with her finger to his lips. "Just do it, Hawke," she said. "We could use all the guid luck we can get."

"All right," he agreed, using both hands to give the cup to

Phoebe to drink first. She took just a sip and gave it back to Hawke. "If I remember correctly, the groom has to finish what's left in the weddin' cup. I'll do that with pleasure," he said, drinking down the rest of the whisky.

"Dinna forget to pay the piper with a dram of whisky as well," said Ethan. "It's what ye're supposed to do."

"Ye are far too superstitious," said Hawke, holding out the cup for Callum to refill it and handing it to Ethan. Ethan smiled and drank it down.

"Now, how about a little food?" Hawke's eyes roamed over to the cooking fires.

"No' yet," said Phoebe.

"That's right," agreed Wren. "Your father wanted to toss the caber before he ate, so the food wouldn't weigh him down.

"Blethers, Mathair. Do we really have to do that now?"

"Here comes the chronicler and his daughter," said Ethan.

"Who invited them?" asked Hawke.

"Caleb did, of course," Ethan replied.

"Your father wanted to make sure they were here as well," said Wren with a smile. "He's mentioned more than once to them that he is the champion of the caber toss."

"Hawke, hurry up. I'm ready," called Storm, standing in the field that would be used to toss the caber.

"Ye are no' goin' to beat me on my own weddin' day," Hawke shouted to his father. Then he looked over to Phoebe. "Kiss me, fast."

"All right," she said, giving him a kiss. "But what was that for?" she asked with a giggle.

"It's for luck."

"I thought ye didna believe in luck and curses," said Ethan. "Or are ye gettin' superstitious, too?"

"Ye're right, I dinna need luck," said Hawke with a shrug and a wink to his wife. "I just wanted to kiss my new bride."

"Hawke, are ye comin'?" shouted his impatient father.

. . .

HAWKE RAN down to the field with everyone following him. He'd be lying to himself if he said he wasn't nervous. All the MacNabs and even the Madmen MacKeefe – his friends' fathers were there. Not to mention, his family, his new children, Phoebe's father and family, and to top it off that danged chronicler and his daughter. The last thing he wanted them to write in that silly book was that he lost a caber toss to his father on his wedding day.

"Hawke, ye go first," said Storm, brushing his hands together. He was the champ at this event. But Hawke was about to beat him, and he wouldn't take it well.

"All right," said Hawke. Logan and Ethan helped him to lift the caber. Hawke concentrated hard to do his best. Tossing the caber, it flipped end over end. The throw was perfect. Everyone cheered and clapped.

"Guid work, Hawke," said Callum, shoving a tankard of whisky in his hand.

"Aye, no' bad," said Storm. "But now I will throw the caber even farther." Storm turned and spoke to the chronicler. "Did ye ken that I have won the caber toss for thirty years now?"

"Thirty years?" asked Bridget, seeming very impressed. "Did ye hear that, Faither?"

"I did," said the chronicler, grasping the book.

"No one has ever beaten me," bragged Storm.

"Until today," Hawke mumbled under his breath. "Go on, Da. Throw the caber. And remember we are only doin' one toss so make it count."

"Son," said Storm with a smile and a shake of his head. "I dinna need more than one throw."

"Storm, just toss the caber so everyone can eat," called out his wife.

Logan and Ethan helped Storm get the caber in place. And

just as he held it up, Apollo landed on top, thinking it was a perch.

"Shoo! Get off of there, ye crazy bird," yelled Storm, wavering back and forth with the pole, trying to get the bird to leave.

"Hawke, are no' ye goin' to call yer bird?" asked Phoebe from next to him.

"Apollo is a free spirit. He'll leave when he's guid and ready," said Hawke with a huge smile, thanking his bird silently.

Then, to make matters even worse for Storm, Caleb's pine marten ran between Storm's legs, almost setting him off balance. The crowd oohed and aahed as Storm almost lost the pole but managed to right the heavy thing again.

Then Ethan's wolfhound and Logan's wolf ran right past Storm on either side, and Caleb was right behind them. "I've almost caught Marty!" shouted Caleb, looking up at Hawke instead of where he was going. "I'll have yer rings back momentarily."

"Caleb, watch out," someone yelled from the crowd.

Caleb stopped short of hitting Storm, holding his hands in the air. "Sorry," he said, and continued to chase after the animals.

With all the distractions, Storm couldn't concentrate. And by the time the hawk flew away, the caber was getting so heavy that his throw was a bad one and not nearly as good as Hawke's.

"Sorry, Storm, but Hawke is the winner," called out Ian from the opposite side of the field, watching how far the poles landed.

"Ye won!" shouted Phoebe, jumping up and down in excitement, kissing Hawke so passionately that he almost got caught up in the moment, wanting to make love to her and forgetting where they were.

"Congratulations, Hawke. Ye will be mentioned in the book," said the chronicler, walking up with his daughter at his side.

Logan and Ethan ran over to join them. Caleb rushed up, holding out his hand.

"Here ye are, Hawke. Two weddin' rings," said Caleb, so out of breath from running that he could barely speak.

Hawke kissed the rings and slipped one onto Phoebe's finger, and let her slide his into place on his hand as well.

"I really feel married now," said Phoebe, holding up her hand to admire the ring in the sun.

"How do ye spell yer name for the chronicles?" asked Bridget.

"With an E at the end," Hawke answered.

"What?" asked Caleb, looking back and forth. "Hawke is gettin' mentioned in the Highland Chronicles? What for?"

"For beatin' me at the caber toss," said Storm, walking over to join them. "Congratulations, Son, even if it wasna a fair competition."

"Now Storm, our son had nothing to do with the distractions," Wren told her husband.

"I'm no' so sure," said Storm, being a sore loser.

"Welcome to the MacNab family, Hawke." Angus MacNab entered the circle of people. "I am proud to call ye my son by marriage."

"I am honored as well, Laird Angus," said Hawke.

Angus continued. "If it wasna for ye comin' to Crookston Castle and fightin' off Euan, Lennox, and the other traitors, I'd be dead right now and so would my daughter. Ye blew through there like a fierce storm. Thank ye." He clasped hands with Hawke. "I dinna think I ever had the chance to thank ye properly for what ye did for us."

"Aye, that was a guid thing ye did, Son," said Storm. "Plus, ye saved yer grandfaither." He slapped Ian on the back. "Of course, I would have been there to do it if I wasna off confrontin' the English."

"I'm yer faither, Storm," Ian reminded him. "Ye couldna have come for me?" He looked at his son sternly.

"Grandda, in my faither's defense, he was servin' the king and he is also a chieftain of the clan," Hawke broke in. "It was his duty to lead our men into battle."

"I suppose so," said Ian.

"Thank ye, Hawke," said Storm with a nod.

"What was that ye said about Hawke fightin' like a storm?" asked Bridget, wanting to get every word to put in the Highland Chronicles.

"He didna fight like a storm," said Hawke's father. And just when Hawke was sure his father was going to tell him that he was the one known for fighting like a storm, Storm surprised him. Putting his hand on Hawke's shoulder, Storm smiled and looked him in the eye. "I am very proud of my son for what he did, riskin' his life when he kent he might no' survive. But I wouldna say he fought like a storm. Nay, that is no' right at all."

"Really?" asked Bridget. "Well, what would ye say?"

"I think that was an understatement and I am officially handing over my title," said Storm. "Because my son, Hawke, did some brave and heroic things, and I'd have to say proudly that he fought like a ***Highland Storm***."

FROM THE AUTHOR

I hoped you enjoyed Hawke and Phoebe's story and will take the time to leave a review for me. Hawke is one of the two sons of Storm MacKeefe, my hero from ***Lady Renegade,*** Book 2 of my ***Legacy of the Blade Series***, if you'd like to read his story as well.

A lot of my books have characters from some of my other series in them. While each book can be read as a stand alone, it is always best to read them in order if possible. I am listing a timeline of some of my medieval series for you.

Timeline of my medieval series:

The Barons of the Cinque Ports

The Baron's Quest - Book 1
The Baron's Bounty - Book 2
The Baron's Destiny - Book 3

* * *

Legacy of the Blade Series:

Legacy of the Blade Prequel
Lord of the Blade - Book 1
Lady Renegade - Book 2
Lord of Illusion - Book 3
Lady of the Mist - Book 4

* * *

Daughters of the Dagger Series:

Daughters of the Dagger Prequel
Ruby - Book 1
Sapphire - Book 2
Amber - Book 3
Amethyst - Book 4

* * *

MadMan MacKeefe Series:

Onyx - Book 1
Aidan - Book 2
Ian - Book 3

* * *

Legendary Bastards of the Crown Series:

Destiny's Kiss - Prequel

Restless Sea Lord - Book 1 ***(Reviewer's Choice - Books and Benches)***

Ruthless Knight - Book 2

Reckless Highlander - Book 3

* * *

Seasons of Fortitude Series:

Highland Spring - Book 1 ***(International Digital Awards Finalist)***

Summer's Reign - Book 2 ***(RONE Award Finalist)***

Autumn's Touch - Book 3

Winter's Flame - Book 4

* * *

Secrets of the Heart Series

Highland Secrets - Book 1 ***(Wishing Well Award Finalist; RONE Award Finalist, Raven Award Finalist)***

Seductive Secrets - Book 2 ***(RONE Award Finalist, Raven Award Finalist, Best Cover Semi-Finalist)***

Rebellious Secrets - Book 3

Forgotten Secrets - Book 4

* * *

Highland Chronicles Series:

Highland Storm – Book 1

Highland Spirit – Book 2

Highland Spy – Book 3

Highland Steel – Book 4

* * *

Here are more:

Second in Command Series: (Secondary Character Romance)
Pirate in the Mist: Brody (Legendary Bastards of the Crown)
Forbidden: Claude (Barons of the Cinque Ports)
Scottish Rose: Coira (MadMan MacKeefe)
Silent Knight: Alexander (Seasons of Fortitude)
Keeper of the Flame: Orrick (Legacy of the Blade)

* * *

Holiday Knights Series: (Medieval Sweet and Clean)
Mistletoe and Chain Mail: Christmas
Matchmade Hearts: Valentine's Day
May Queen: May Day

* * *

A Look Behind the Series:
Behind the Chain Mail (Legendary Bastards of the Crown) w/Bonus book, The Gift

Watch for Hawke's friend, Ethan's story coming next in ***Highland Spirit*** to find out more about the haunted castle on the isle. And if you'd like to read Orrick's story, who is the sorcerer first seen in my ***Legacy of the Blade Series***, his book will be ***Keeper of the Flame*** – Book 5 in my ***Second in Command Series***.

Happy reading!

Elizabeth Rose

ABOUT ELIZABETH

Elizabeth Rose is a multi-published, bestselling author, writing medieval, historical, contemporary, paranormal, and western romance. Her books are available as EBooks, paperbacks, and audiobooks as well.

Her favorite characters in her works include dark, dangerous and tortured heroes, and feisty, independent heroines who know how to wield a sword. She loves writing 14th century medieval novels, and is well-known for her many series.

Her twelve-book small town contemporary series, Tarnished Saints, was inspired by incidents in her own life.

After being traditionally published, she started self-publishing, creating her own covers and book trailers on a dare from her two sons.

Elizabeth loves the outdoors. In the summertime, you can find her in her secret garden with her laptop, swinging in her hammock working on her next book. Elizabeth is a born storyteller and passionate about sharing her works with her readers.

Please be sure to visit her website at **Elizabethrosenovels.com** to read excerpts from any of her novels and get sneak peeks at covers of upcoming books. You can follow her on **Twitter, Facebook**, **Goodreads** or **BookBub.** Be sure to sign up for her **newsletter** so you don't miss out on new releases or upcoming events.

ALSO BY ELIZABETH ROSE

Medieval

Legendary Bastards of the Crown Series

Seasons of Fortitude Series

Secrets of the Heart Series

Legacy of the Blade Series

Daughters of the Dagger Series

MadMan MacKeefe Series

Barons of the Cinque Ports Series

Second in Command Series

Holiday Knights Series

Highland Chronicles Series

Medieval/Paranormal

Elemental Magick Series

Greek Myth Fantasy Series

Tangled Tales Series

Contemporary

Tarnished Saints Series

Working Man Series

Western

Cowboys of the Old West Series

And more!

Please visit http://elizabethrosenovels.com

Elizabeth Rose

Made in the USA
Lexington, KY
14 September 2019